VALERIE WILSON WESLEY

THE DEVIL RIDING

AVON BOOKS
An Imprint of HarperCollins*Publishers*

AVON BOOKS
An Imprint of HarperCollinsPublishers
10 East 53rd Street
New York, New York 10022-5299

Copyright © 2000 by Valerie Wilson Wesley
ISBN: 0-380-73208-4
www.avonmystery.com

Excerpt from "Arkansas Chant" from *The Collected Poems of Sterling A. Brown*, edited by Michael S. Harper. Copyright © 1980 by Sterling A. Brown. Reprinted by permission of HarperCollins Publishers, Inc.

First Avon Books paperback printing: May 2002

Avon Trademark Reg. U.S. Pat. Off. and in Other Countries, Marca Registrada, Hecho en U.S.A.
HarperCollins® is a trademark of HarperCollins Publishers Inc.

Printed in the U.S.A.

10 9 8 7 6 5 4 3 2 1

Resounding acclaim for
VALERIE WILSON WESLEY's
TAMARA HAYLE

"A welcome new voice and a fresh point of view."
USA Today

"There's a richness of language in Wesley's writing, joined by a delightful sense of humor. She makes the mean streets of Newark come alive."
San Francisco Examiner

"Tamara Hayle isn't just Sue Grafton's PI Kinsey Milhone or Sara Paretsky's V.I. Warshawski with a little more melanin. She's a thirtysomething sister with her own walk, talk, and impudent wit from a rich black experience."
Dallas Morning News

"Tamara's sassy voice is so entertaining."
Washington Post Book World

"Tamara is a wonderfully believable and independent sleuth who combines intelligence and intuition, sexiness and self-control, and tenderness and toughness, all sometimes in a single scene."
Denver Post

"Wesley is a smooth, gifted practitioner of her art. Walk down any city street and you'll meet her characters; talk to them and they'll use Wesley's words . . . Sue Grafton, Janet Evanovich, Raymond Chandler, Walter Mosley—Wesley joins them with flair."
Greensboro News & Record

I'd like to thank Norma Lewis-Totah for sharing her expertise, and Jacqueline Preston for showing me around her town. Again, my gratitude for their suggestions and insights to all of my "first readers"—Joy Cain, Regina Waynes Joseph, Janet Taylor Pickett, Mary Jackson Scroggins, Rosemarie Robotham, and Charlotte Wiggers. As usual, my thanks to my agent, Faith H. Childs, and my editor, Stacy Creamer. And as always, to Richard, my love.

For my nephew, Cheo Hodari Coker,
who has always loved a good gangsta story

The rider is a devil
And there's hell to pay;
The Devil is a rider,
God may be the owner
But he's rich and forgetful
And far away.

"Arkansas Chant"
—*Sterling A. Brown*

THE DEVIL RIDING

It was half past midnight on a Friday night—the witching hour, my dead grandma used to call it. I was tending bar in a gangster's suite in a glitzy Atlantic City hotel. I'd stuffed myself into a black silk sheath as snug as it was expensive and was pouring drinks, grinning like a fool. But I was scared.

I was looking for a young runaway named Gabriella Desmond whose rich parents had paid me serious money to find out where she'd run. The trail had led me here but the girl didn't want to be found so I had to earn my money the hard way—with tact and discretion. No P.I. license flashed. No probing questions. At least not yet.

I hadn't looked for many runaways, but the few cases I'd taken had turned out well. There had been a troubled little druggie from Essex Fells whom I'd helped get into rehab; an angry ten-year-old whose recently remarried mama forgot to tell him that she loved him; a smart-mouthed Newark teen whose tough-talking daddy cried like a baby when he held her in his arms again. They had all been found easily and in predictable places: a sympathetic friend's bedroom, a deserted basement, a video parlor, a fast-food joint. They'd come home easily and been welcomed by parents who swore they'd mend their ways and never let them leave again.

I had my doubts about this new one, though. Gabriella Desmond had taken off the first week in November. It was March now, and her trail was decidedly cold. She was eighteen years old and whatever had chased her away would probably chase her again if she wasn't yet ready to face it down. I had my doubts about the Desmonds, too—why they waited so long to call me, if they had told me the whole truth, how they would treat her if she actually came back. But I had no doubt that the girl was in more danger than she could possibly know. She'd run to a fun-loving city in dangerous times, and she was young, pretty and rich, a combination that will make a victim out of a woman quicker than hot grease catches fire. And there was a killer on the streets. There was no doubt about that, either.

His victims were young prostitutes, runaways mostly, who were likely to have had a passing acquaintance. The murders were brutal, ruthless and all committed near the end of the week. The first woman had been murdered on the first Friday in November, and there had been four since then, one killing a month. The murder scenes had been wiped clean, with no souvenirs taken or brutal signatures left to bait the cops and feed some sick, sadistic hunger. The women had been beaten to death and their bodies discovered well after the fact, tucked out of the way in hidden places. At least that had been the case up until the most recent victim, who'd been found in her own home, suggesting, perhaps, that this killer was changing directions, growing bolder with his success.

Folks had started to grumble that the police weren't doing enough because the murder victims were poor and black or Latino, so nobody in high places really gave a damn one way or the other. But the fifth girl was white. Her name was Layne Grimaldi and, like two of the others, she had been killed on a Friday, but she had been found in the apartment she shared with another young woman—Gabriella Desmond. At their lawyer's suggestion, the Desmonds called me the Saturday after Layne's body was found and hired me the following Monday. They were afraid their

3

runaway daughter might be the next victim, and they were determined to find her before the murderer struck again.

The first few days in town, I'd visited the traditional places homeless teenagers hide: Covenant House, the boardwalk, fast-food restaurants offering cheap food and video games. I'd had no luck, and it was time to go in another direction. My good friend Jake, a public defender, put me in touch with a hotel manager who owed him a favor, and the man had arranged for me to tend bar at a high-stakes poker game thrown for big-time players and small-time hoods. The host was a man named Delmundo Real and the manager hinted that if I kept my eyes open and mouth shut I might find a lead on Gabriella. Pretty young girls with nowhere to go routinely decorated Real's parties, so if Gabriella was still in town chances were she'd show up there. At worst, I might come across someone who'd crossed paths with her. The manager also warned me that if anything bad went down I'd be on my own. I'd given him a tough-girl shrug and told him I could take care of myself. Truth was, I wasn't so sure.

But I'd been in the party since nine, and although my hands were shaking when I mixed the drinks, nobody seemed to notice my fear. Straight scotch or gin and juice were the cocktails of the hour, and I poured them fast and free. I kneeled down to pick up a napkin a drunk had aimed at the trash can behind me when a young woman sauntered up to the bar and requested a drink.

"Amaretto. Neat," she said in a baby-soft voice.

"Neat?" I stood up to face her. She was dressed in a short red dress that was tighter than mine, which was saying something that shouldn't be said. Her hair was piled high on her head and glossy black curls cascaded into a face that, despite too much makeup, looked younger than she wanted folks to know. But her bright eyes had a hard edge, as if they'd already taken in more than they were meant to.

"That means straight, which means nothing in it." She gave me a patronizing smile.

"I know what 'neat' means, but you're too young to have it neat, sweet or anything else." I sounded like somebody's mother, which I am. She tipped her head to the side as if trying to figure out how to get around me. I'd seen that gesture before; it was one of my son's.

"How old are you anyway?" I asked her.

She studied me for a moment. "Old enough to fuck without getting stuck."

"That one's as old as me," I said, without missing a beat. "But whatever you do or don't get stuck doing, honey, you're stuck tonight with a soft drink because I have no intention of serving you liquor." I picked a towel off the edge of the bar and polished one of the glasses, keeping an eye on the girl from the mirror behind me. She scowled like my son does when something doesn't go his way, then sunk down on a barstool with a thud. I poured her a Coke, stuck a lemon slice on the top of the glass and slid it across to her.

She glanced at the drink critically and then at me. "You know if I *really* wanted a drink all I'd have to do is ask one of them suckas over there, and he'd get me one just like that." She snapped her long, red-nailed fingers to emphasize her point. Pouring a diet Coke for myself, I settled down on the stool behind the bar so we'd be eye to eye.

She looked me over, then gave me a hesitant smile that said I'd passed whatever test she was giving. "So how long you been tending bar?"

"About as long as you been walking this earth."

"So how long you think that is?"

"About sixteen years," I said, and the shy half-grin that pushed itself out on her lips told me I'd guessed right. "So why is a girl as young and pretty as you hanging around a place like this?" I asked her, even though I suspected the answer.

She shrugged prettily then asked, "So where you think I should be?"

"Well, when I was your age, I was—"

"Lady, you were *never* my age," she said in a way that told me she'd seen things in her sixteen years most people twice her age never want to. But I also suspected she wasn't as hard as she wanted me to think, and if she was on the street now she hadn't been there long. I also noticed her earrings, which were tiny pearls encased in gold, and out of place with her dress and ostentatious hairdo. They were earrings that looked as if they had been selected with care, a first piece of jewelry for a baby with newly pierced ears or a young girl breaking into womanhood. I wondered how long ago they'd been given to her. Her gaze shifted as if she could read my thoughts, and her eyes roamed the room.

We were in a penthouse suite, the highest thing in a hotel called the Sultan's Lair, which like Caesars Palace, the Taj Mahal and nearly every other hotel in Atlantic City was tarted up to look like something it wasn't. Aging women decked out as belly dancers served drinks and snacks from gilded trays. Old men in Bedouin robes and turbans carried bags and pushed suitcases on trolleys. Although this suite, called the Sultan's Tent, might cost a king's ransom, no self-respecting sultan would be caught dead in it. In this world of bad manners and worse taste it was the tackiest place I'd seen yet.

The glossy off-white walls were trimmed with

gold leaf and the long, narrow white couch slung low against the wall was upholstered in velvet more suited to a teddy bear's rump. A thick gold shag carpet, which should have gone out with the sixties, covered the floor. Molded columns stood against walls topped by high ceilings studded with tiny glittering stars. There were at least four bedrooms in the suite, all had arched doors trimmed in paper ivy; all the doors were closed. Every so often, a man, accompanied by a woman half his age and girth, would quietly exit to one of these bedrooms.

But the real action was around the four mahogany card tables in the center of the room. The game was poker, played fast and furiously, and the exhilaration that comes with losing easy money hard permeated the room like a heady perfume. It was simple to see why this kid would be fascinated. A sly smile appeared on her lips as she gazed around the room. One of the men beckoned her with a diamond-ringed index finger. She tossed him a saucy grin, raised her drink in salute and turned back to me.

"So what's your name?" she asked.

"Tommie Hayes." I gave her the fake one I'd scribbled on the hotel register. "What's yours?"

"Amaretta. My mama named me after that drink except it's with an A. It was her favorite drink, and she used to put it in milk to make me go to sleep when I was a baby."

Was her mother dead? Had she been the kind of woman who would give her baby liquor to put her to sleep? "Amaretta. That's a very pretty name."

She took a gulp of her Coke, and her gaze traveled the room as if she were looking for somebody who wasn't there. They finally came to rest on a man on the far side of the room who slouched down in a chair. His long legs were crossed and there was an enigmatic smile on his full lips. He was very tall, bone thin and impeccably dressed in a conservative charcoal-gray suit. His tawny brown skin was as clear as a child's, and his curly jet-black hair was pulled back in a short, silky ponytail. He wore no jewelry save a gold stud in his right ear. His eyes turned in my direction and fastened on me, like an animal does when it knows it's being watched. He smiled shyly, shifted his attention to Amaretta, then lazily stood up and ambled toward us. Amaretta picked up her drink and sipped it, but her eyes never left him. He turned abruptly and went into one of the rooms, leaving the door ajar. I didn't realize she was holding her breath until she let it go.

"Who is that?" I asked her.

"Don't you know who that is? He hired you, didn't he?" Her eyes focused on me suspiciously.

9

"The manager hired me. I'm covering for somebody. The usual girl had an emergency, and she had to split. It's okay."

"That's Del. Delmundo Real." She eyed me warily while she finished her Coke. I poured her another, put some mixed nuts in a glass bowl and placed them in front of her. "How high up you think we are?" she asked, deciding that maybe she could trust me.

"About thirty stories." I sat back down on my stool.

"When it gets warm you can stand out there on that balcony and see the waves hit the beach and go back out again." She ate a few nuts, dabbed at her mouth with a napkin, then took out a compact, checked her teeth and spread on some lipstick. Her eyes met mine again. "The ocean takes everything with it. Shells. Trash. I even saw it pick up a kitten once, swept it out to sea." She shook her head very slightly as if trying to shake out the memory. "Sometimes I stand up here and wish I could ride out there with it, let it take me anywhere it wants to. Never look back."

"How far would you like to go, Amaretta?" *Where had she come from and why was she afraid to go back?*

"A girl fell off the balcony last summer." She changed the subject, her voice hushed. "Her name was LaTisha. The cops say she jumped but people say somebody pushed her."

"Did you know her?" I watched her closely.

She shrugged as if to say that she didn't, but something in her eyes and in the way she moved her shoulders told me that she did.

"What do you think happened to her?" I tried to read what she was afraid to say.

"Do you have any kids?" She changed the subject again, and I wondered what it would take to make her open up.

"Yeah. A son, about your age. Maybe a year or two younger."

"You don't look old enough to have a kid my age."

"I'm like you, Amaretta, older than I look," I said, only half-joking, and she smiled like she appreciated the joke.

"Where is he?" She turned serious again.

"My son? Home. Probably watching TV. Supposed to be doing his homework."

"Don't let Del know you have a kid. He likes the women who work for him to be free. Be convenient." She added those last two words with a laugh that wasn't one and tugged at my heart.

"So how long have you been 'convenient,' Amaretta?" I turned serious, and she avoided my eyes so I went in another direction. "Did you know the girl who was killed last Friday? Layne Grimaldi." She was still too young to hide what was in her eyes. I picked up a glass and pretended to polish it. "Was she convenient?" The shrug she gave indicated that Layne Grimaldi wasn't, and I wondered if she had talked to the police. "Do you know a girl named Gabriella Desmond?"

Her voice was steady when she answered, but her eyes got so big and innocent I knew she must be lying. "Gabriella Desmond? No, I don't think so." But the tenderness in her voice when she said Gabriella's name told me she might be trying to protect her, and if her voice hadn't said it, the way she finished off her soda, abruptly stood and left without another word or glance at me told me what I wanted to know. I watched her as she headed for the room where Delmundo Real had gone, and before she entered she turned around and gave me a look filled with anguish.

Angry at myself and distracted, I washed glasses without seeing them. I'd blown it, and I wondered how I could have played it differently. I poured drinks, polished glasses and argued with myself for the next hour or so and wondered how I could talk to her again and what I would say to her when I did.

I'm not sure what made me look up or how long he had been standing there, but my heart stopped the moment I laid eyes on him. The last time I'd seen him he lay bleeding on a terrace in the Blue Mountains of Jamaica. I was afraid he was dying. Later that year, flowers came to mark the anniversary of our last meeting, and I knew then what I should have known all along. Men like Basil Dupre don't leave this life easily, not before they're good and ready to go.

He has always strolled into my life when I least expect to see him, like some delightful cosmic gift sent to remind me that there's more to me than Jamal's mother, Annie's friend, the sole family survivor who remembers her dead. I have always been mystified and often disturbed by my feelings for him—how deep they go, how starkly sexual they are, how quickly they make me forget my good sense. I can count on one hand the number of times we've been together, yet each encounter has fed some lingering hunger that I didn't know I had. Every time I see him, I forget how long it has been.

He is remarkably handsome in the way that black men can be: high, fine cheekbones and full lips that are clearly African with a suggestion of Arawak Indian; dark skin that glows as if a sun burned from within; enough self-confidence (which some probably call arrogance) to take over any room he steps into; sensuality brushed with a hint of danger and unpredictability as unsettling as it is fascinating.

He glanced in my direction, his eyes widened slightly when he saw me but there was no other change in his expression. Basil Dupre is a man of controlled response, a survivor in a treacherous world where taking risks is all that counts and pure instinct can save or take a life. His eyes assessed the scene that he had stepped into and came back to me, acknowledging me with a nod, but his eyes expressed concern, that I could clearly see. I glanced away quickly, not able to trust my response.

Several people came forward to greet him, and as always with "business" associates he was distant, formal. Someone beckoned him toward a card game that was beginning, and he gave a smile that indicated he might join. A plump, pink-faced man in an ill-fitting suit nodded almost imperceptibly toward the room where Amaretta had gone, and a look that I couldn't read crossed Basil's face. A model-thin woman with long reddish hair embraced him, seductively pushing her body into his, but his mind was still on the room with the closed door, and he glanced toward it and then at me over the woman's head. He gently but firmly took her arms from around his neck and came toward me. I concentrated on polishing a champagne glass.

There were several people at the bar when he reached it, and he stood near for a while, biding his time until they left. I could feel his eyes upon me, but I avoided looking at him because I knew mine would give me away. He leaned toward me, touched my hand to get my attention, and that small, tender gesture sent a tremor of excitement through me. But the word he spoke chilled me to my bones.

"Beware," he said.

2

In the beginning, there seemed to be nothing to fear. It was the second week in March, and it felt like spring the morning I met the Desmonds. I was carefree and self-confident. They were high-paying clients that Sam Henderson, an attorney I know, had tossed my way, and I was glad to still be in his good graces. He hadn't told me much about them except they were influential and rich, but I would have known that the moment I drove up to the house. It was perched on the highest hill in lofty Belvington Heights and looked like some venerable antebellum plantation, yet it was strangely devoid of character or charm. Unwilling for the sputter and wheeze of the Blue Demon—my ancient diesel Jetta—to announce my arrival, I parked at the far end of the long driveway and walked to the door. But I was uneasy as I rang the bell. For one thing, the closer I got to the place the less I liked the look of it. The pale color, baroque trim and lush grounds evoked racial memories of "The Big House" where the seeds of my forebears were definitely *not* sown.

A small-boned, caramel-colored woman in gray tweed and cashmere opened the door. Against my will, my eyes dropped to the two-carat diamond ring that sparkled on her left hand. Its ornate setting was too heavy for her finger. After a moment of awkward silence, I managed to pick up my eyes and paste on my obsequious, servant-at-your-service, professional smile.

"Good morning, Mrs. Desmond. I'm Tamara Hayle, the private investigator Sam Henderson recommended." She looked puzzled so I added, "You called me Saturday morning."

"Oh yes, of course. I'm Dominique Desmond. Please come in." Her voice was deep with just a hint of the South. I stepped inside, pausing at the door to take in the house. An elegant staircase flowed down the center of the hall, cutting the house in half, but the place had a musty smell, as if it needed a good airing, even though it was probably cleaned and polished daily by unseen, underpaid hands. The high ceilings were edged with elaborate trim, and the black-and-white tiled floor shone like mirrors. A twinkling chandelier hung high from the ceiling and caught the bright morning sun. But the place had an oppressive, gloomy feel about it that made me uncomfortable. She briskly led me through the house without speaking. Being naturally nosy, I tried to glimpse the various rooms as we swept past but couldn't see much except a smattering of Oriental rugs and heavy furniture. The place was as hushed and still as a tomb; our footsteps echoed from the walls.

She opened an oak door that led into a room that looked like it had once been a library, although there were no books on the shelves. It was a small room, and embers from an earlier fire still glowed in the fireplace, but the fire must have died before it gave any warmth. An elaborately framed portrait of a man in his late fifties hung above the fireplace. He was dressed in a severe black suit, the kind that an undertaker wears, which contrasted sharply with his pale skin. His hair, which was close-cropped and speckled with gray, identified him as a black man. His expression was aloof, almost cold, and his eyes looked hollow. I wondered if the lack of warmth had been there in life or was simply the artist's lack of skill. He looked familiar, and I wondered where and when I had seen him before.

Dominique Desmond sank down into a leather chair beside the fireplace as if she were out of breath, and indicated that I should sit on the matching couch across from her. She was much younger than I initially thought, mid-thirties maybe, not close to forty. Her long black hair was pulled off her face in a tight chignon that emphasized her high cheekbones and delicate features. But her dark eyes were filled with woe. I reached into my Kenya bag for my black-and-white notebook and felt-tipped pen, and sat at attention, poised and ready for her to begin.

"I've called you because of what happened three days ago, last Friday, about the girl who was murdered in Atlantic City. About the serial killer," she said.

"They're not completely sure if the killings are serial," I said with an ex-cop's caution, but I wondered what it had to do with her.

"It doesn't matter one way or the other to me, if they're serial or not, but it's the girl who was killed, Layne Grimaldi, who concerns me."

"You knew her?" I was surprised, and my voice showed it.

"My daughter did. The girl was her roommate. My daughter has disappeared. Her name is Gabriella Desmond. She is eighteen years old, and she ran away on November fourth, four months ago. I don't know where she is. I want you to find her." She spoke quickly, her voice even, her eyes staring straight ahead, and I jotted the facts down quickly, trying to make sense enough of it to put things in order.

"If she ran away four months ago, and you don't know where she is, how do you know that she was living with the dead girl?" I asked the obvious.

She answered without a pause. "Before the girl was murdered, I got a call from somebody who left me the number of the apartment. The person said I could reach my daughter there, and when I called, I spoke to the dead girl, Layne Grimaldi. She said that Gabriella was staying there, and that she would tell her to call me, but I never heard from either of them again." Her face grew troubled, and she sighed a long, uneasy sigh.

"Was the person who called you and gave you the number a woman or a man?"

"A woman. A very young one, I think."

"How long ago did she call?"

"Last month, in early February."

"And you haven't heard from anybody since?"

"No."

"So you really don't know if Gabriella was still living with Layne Grimaldi when she was murdered?"

"No. But something tells me that my daughter is in danger." She paused for a moment, as if wondering if she should say something else and then added, "Do you have any children, Ms. Hayle?"

"Yes, I do."

"Do you believe in mother's intuition?" I nodded because I knew what she was talking about. "I can feel it in my bones, in my heart. I know that my daughter needs me."

"Have the police contacted you yet? If she was rooming with the girl, they need to talk to her."

"I haven't heard from them, so maybe she moved out and left no forwarding address. Maybe she wasn't there. I just know that she needs me." She shook her head in frustration, and dropped her eyes.

"What did the police say when you first reported her missing?"

"We never reported her missing. My husband didn't feel it was necessary. He said it would brand her as a runaway and everybody would know she was a troubled child," she said.

I shifted my gaze to the portrait above the fireplace so she couldn't see how shocked I was, and when I looked back at her I asked, "Is there anything that happened the week she left that would have made her go? An argument, maybe? My son threatens to run away from home at least once a month." I added the last bit with a hint of a smile, reassuring her that the same thing could happen to me or any other mother. But it was a lie. There has never been that much anger between me and my son. We argue, make up, argue again but never stay mad for long. For one thing, Jamal likes knowing where his next meal is coming from too much to leave home for more than a couple of hours. Besides that, we've both suffered too many losses to ever forget that we're the only thing the other one has, and that makes for strong love and a sense of vulnerability. We have never taken each other for granted.

"Nothing happened out of the ordinary," Dominique continued. "But my daughter has always been . . . troubled. As a child she was difficult, and she continues to be. She's had problems adjusting ever since I remarried." She went to a table on the other side of the room, brought back a photograph of her daughter and handed it to me. Gabriella Desmond bore a striking resemblance to her mother, except for her hair, which was cut in a spiky punk cut, and her skin, which was a richer brown.

"When you say 'difficult,' what do you mean?" I handed the photograph back.

"Cutting school. Bad grades. Acting out. Smoking. Drinking. Hanging out with the wrong kids." She studied the photo for a moment, smiled like I do when I look at photographs of my son, then brought it to her lips and kissed it. "She is my heart," she said. "I love her more than I love anything in this world. She is my heart."

Her love and anguish touched me, and my feelings toward her softened. Yet I couldn't make this expression of maternal devotion fit with the carelessness of a woman who didn't report her teenage daughter missing because her ole man told her not to.

"Could she have run off with friends? These 'wrong kids' you mentioned?" She hesitated just long enough to tell me what she would say was important. "She has a friend. I think she called him Rook. I've only seen him once, and that was just his back, a couple of months before she ran off. They were walking down the street together."

"How did you know they were together?"

She paused for a moment. "They were holding hands."

"What did you say to her when she got home?"

"I forbade her to see him."

"Why?"

"He made me uncomfortable."

"Why did he make you uncomfortable?"

"The way he was dressed. The way he carried himself. He had a lope to the way he walked, like a wolf."

"His name was Rook?"

"That's what she called him."

"When did she meet him?"

"A while ago. I don't know where he's from, but I think she met him on the boardwalk in Atlantic City. He's a runaway, homeless teenager, I think. Very pathetic. She stayed in our home down there last summer, and I think she met him then."

"Do you think she ran away to be with him?"

"As far as I know, they haven't seen each other since."

"And you have no idea why she left?"

She began to cry softly. "I should, but I don't."

I let her regain her composure before I continued, making my voice as sympathetic as I could. "You said Gabriella has been difficult since you remarried. How long ago was that?"

"Foster and I married nine years ago. She had just turned nine, only a few years younger than my stepson."

"And how does she get along with your stepson?"

"There was some tension at first, but then they became very close, extremely close, as close as if they'd been blood. But he's everything she's not." Her bluntness surprised me, and she didn't elaborate. But since she'd said the girl was troubled I assumed her stepson was a paragon of obedience and virtue. The good child vs. the bad one. I'd seen

that situation often enough, but when it comes to
kids, good and bad are always relative terms.

"What is your stepson's name?"

"Carver. Carver Desmond," she said, and as I
wrote the name down, it all came back: who they
were, what they had done, why they were important. I glanced again at the stern portrait over the
fireplace, annoyed with Sam Henderson for not
letting me know who I'd be working for. He probably didn't want me to be intimidated, and if that
was the case, he was right because I was.

I'd heard the name Carver Desmond, for whom
her stepson had been named, for as long as I could
remember, and the facts of his life now came back
to me. Carver Desmond had made a fortune by
the time he was twenty-five. He took a funeral
parlor inherited from his father and turned it into
a chain of establishments where black folks could
bury their dead cheaply and respectably. *Desmond
with Dignity* had been his motto, and it had been
inscribed on countless church fans, Sunday school
programs and Ladies' Aid brochures in poor black
neighborhoods all across the state. I still had the
one my grandmother kept wedged into a corner
of her mirror on her ancient vanity table. God
knew how often she'd visited his homes to bid
close friends good-bye. Black people died harder
and faster than anybody else in those days, and

most white morticians balked at handling their remains. Truth was, even if white men deigned to do it, family members preferred the last earthly hands to touch their loved ones *not* be the color of those that had snatched away so much in life. And that was where Carver Desmond stepped in. He had built his fortune on black grief and white hatred. From his funeral homes had flowed real estate, bought cheap and sold high to families just up from the South. From that came the restaurants that served food as cheap as those places run by Daddy Grace without the religion. There were the hotels, where a black man could sleep the night and know he could sit in the parlor. Carver Desmond made a fortune during segregation and spent it like few black men have before or since.

He'd never married but had grown old supporting a twin sister named Ida and a kid brother years younger. Ida Desmond had been one of the first black socialites in the state. Her stomping grounds had been Atlantic City and Asbury Park. She played the social game harder and meaner than any other black woman before her, creating the clubs, setting the standards, making the rules others were glad to follow. And if her rules had been about anything, they had been about class and color. They had also been about money. Old Negro money. And here I sat in the midst of it.

I stole another look at Dominique Desmond, trying to figure out where and how she fit in. "So Gabriella was adopted by your husband?"

"Yes."

"And your husband's full name again?"

"Foster Desmond."

The younger brother.

"Carver Desmond was my late brother-in-law. Miss Ida Desmond was dead long before I came into the picture or I probably wouldn't have come into it." She said it as if she could read my mind, but I was struck by the strain in her voice, as if she'd explained it all before.

"Is Gabriella's natural father still alive?"

"Yes."

"Does he live in this area?"

"No, in South Jersey. Atlantic City. As I said before, our family, the Desmonds, have a summer place there. I'm from there originally, too. It's where I met Foster. But I rarely go there now. My husband sometimes stays there when he goes to Atlantic City on business."

"I assume you've checked that home to make sure your daughter isn't hiding there?"

"We have a live-in housekeeper, and she hasn't reported anything unusual. I gave the number of that house to the girl who called, and told her to leave a message for me with that housekeeper if she had to talk to me and couldn't reach me here. But I don't think Gabriella would go there. It would be the first place we'd look."

"Have you contacted her father? Maybe Gabriella is living with him."

"She's not. We had our attorney check."

"And what is her natural father's name?" She didn't answer for a while, and I sat poised and waiting, pen in hand.

"Gabriel Wallace. The . . . community activist," she said.

"Community activist?" I put my pen down and tried to make my voice sound neutral, but my amazement at her understatement was clear. Unlike the Desmond surname, I recognized his name at once. Gabriel Wallace was the only black member of a right-wing, right-to-life group linked to the attempted bombings of women's health clinics in poor black neighborhoods around the state. He was loud, self-righteous and annoying, the first to grab a mike, thrust himself in front of a camera and scream about the killing of black babies in the "clinics of doom." And he didn't limit himself to "protecting the unborn." He routinely vowed to "protect" the rest of us from the "undesirables around us" who could end up being anybody from an AIDS patient to a homeless person to a drug-addicted teenage prostitute. His white three-piece suit was always immaculate. He spoke in pretentious, comical tones, but his words were deadly. *How had Dominique Desmond started there and ended up here?* I wondered, and I asked her finally as tactfully and cautiously as I could. She explained, avoiding my eyes.

"Gabriel and I were very young when we married. Just teenagers, not that much older than Gabriella is now. Our marriage was a bad one, very destructive, very ugly. And no. My politics do not reflect his and never have. I've kept my daughter separate from him, protected her. Gabriel Wallace is not part of our lives, and he hasn't been for at least seven years."

"But she knows how to get in touch with him."

"I assume she does," she said, with a testy edge I hadn't seen before. "But he said he hadn't seen her."

I made a note to call their attorney and ask him to put me in touch with Mr. Wallace. "Is there anything else you can think of to tell me about Gabriella?"

She looked lost for a moment, and then shook her head helplessly to indicate that there wasn't. "Then you will take my case?" She asked as if she were actually afraid that I wouldn't. But there was no question what my answer would be. Broke as I was and always seemed to be, I didn't have a choice. And despite myself and her occasionally troubling behavior, her sorrow had touched me. I assured her that I would.

"Should I report my findings directly to you?" I asked my final, practical question as I put my pen and notebook back into my bag. She looked puzzled so I explained. "Is your husband involved in this search as well? Or would you like me to use . . . discretion?" You can never be sure with rich folks who is keeping what secret from whom, and her husband's hesitation about her calling the police in the first place puzzled me. Besides that, Henderson hadn't said exactly *who* was hiring me, and since she was the only one I'd spoken to I needed a clear understanding of who was paying my fee. The answer to my question came quickly.

"I have advised my wife about how I feel, but she insists upon continuing this so I am forced to support her," said a commanding voice from the door. Startled, I turned around to face two men, obviously father and son. The younger man took a seat beside me on the couch, and the older, whom I assumed was Foster Desmond, stood behind his wife's chair, his hand resting possessively on her shoulder. The men had obviously come from a health club, and both were dressed in navy sweats and Nike sneakers and carried identical leather gym bags. They had the same coloring and general facial structure as Carver Desmond the Famous and they were about the same height, but Foster was plump and his shoulders had a womanish curve to them.

"I'm Foster Desmond," he said as if I hadn't guessed. I introduced myself and shook his hand, which was damp and clung to mine much longer than it needed to. "My daughter has disappeared and I really don't think we should put any pressure on her to return home until she's ready to live by the rules. I think she's just pulling one of her pranks, but my wife wants you to look for her and so you should," he said in a refined but authoritative voice that left no doubt as to who was in charge. "You come with good references," he added, as if I'd applied for a job as the downstairs maid.

"Thank you very much," I said. I have never responded well to authority. I forced a smile. He walked over to the far side of the room, opened a mahogany cabinet that concealed a small refrigerator, took out a small blue bottle of water and gulped it down.

"I'd like you to start looking in Atlantic City, where she was last seen. That will probably be where she will be found." He wiped his mouth with the towel that was around his neck.

"Yes. That probably is the best place to start," I said, agreeably.

"All your bills—hotel, food, travel expenses—should be sent directly to our attorney, who will handle the payment of your fees as well. I will instruct him to set aside a special account in one of our banks for you to draw from if you need cash for any reason, but you must be able to justify its use or it will be deducted from your final fee. Tell him anything you find out, and he will relay the message to me. There's no need for you to contact us directly again." I glanced at his wife, who sat very stiffly and stared straight ahead.

"That sounds fine," I said with a tight, proper smile. Men who feel the need to dominate a room are usually weak. Foster Desmond's strut told me more about his character than he knew. He glanced at his watch. I took the hint.

"It will be my pleasure to serve you both," I said with a twinge of self-disgust at how shamelessly the prospect of big money will make me grovel. With a benevolent nod in my general direction and with no further word to anyone, Foster Desmond stepped from the room. Dominique remained seated, silent and stiff in her chair.

As I rose to leave, the son, whom I had all but forgotten, stood and touched my hand, and I glanced up at him. He extended his hand toward me, and I shook it, surprised by the strength of his grip, which was so unlike his father's.

"May I walk you to your car?" His tone was formal, but he stuttered slightly, which softened the impact, but his shy yet eager smile was welcomed after his father's condescension. As we walked through the house, I wondered what additional information I could pump from him on the way to the car. But he walked quickly, staring directly in front of him, seemingly lost in his thoughts.

The sun was shining brightly when we stepped outside, and he paused for a moment and squinted up at it, staring hard at it as if trying to pull some of its warmth into his body. Then he turned and slammed the door hard behind him, as if shutting something out or keeping something in. He smiled at me shyly when he noticed my curious glance.

"I hate this house," he said, as if explaining his actions.

I tried not to look surprised. "Really? It's really quite something. How long has your family lived here?"

"Forever."

"Do you have your own place?"

"No."

"You just hang out with friends as much as you can," I suggested as if I were wise to the ways of young men.

"No. I spend as much time as I can at our place in South Jersey. Near Atlantic City. It used to belong to my aunt. Aunt Ida." Since leaving the house he had become visibly relaxed, his hands dangled at his sides. We walked a bit farther without talking.

"So have you heard from your sister?" I asked conspiratorially as we turned the bend leading to my car. His statement about his home hinted that there might be tension with his parents, and I wondered if there was a chance he'd heard from Gabriella even though they hadn't.

"Stepsister," he quickly corrected me. "No. I haven't seen her." He spoke curtly, as if trying to avoid any more questions.

But I pushed on anyway. "Do you want to hear from her?"

"Why do you ask that?" He shifted his eyes to the ground.

"Has she ever mentioned a friend of hers to you. A guy named Rook."

"Yeah."

"What's his real name?"

"Cardell. Cardell Cummings."

"Where does he live?"

"Nowhere, as far as I can tell."

"How old is he?"

"Same age as Gaby."

"Does he have parents?"

"He doesn't come from anything."

"Tell me about him."

"He's just a nigger, that's all," he said. "Nothing but a nigger. That's her taste in men."

I was stunned by the use of that word, which I will always hate, despite the casualness with which some young black men like to say it. It's still a fighting word to me, and my reply to him showed it.

"What do you mean by that?"

"You don't know what a nigger is?"

"No. I'm afraid I don't."

"Ask my sister when you find her. She'll tell you," he added with a smirk.

"I take it the two of you aren't close."

"Close enough," he said. We walked a bit farther, and then he added, "Mothers can get too protective, sometimes. It causes trouble." I wasn't sure whose mother he was talking about, but I assumed he was talking about Dominique and her concern for Gabriella.

"I have such admiration for your uncle. You must be very proud of your family," I said, taking a stab at flattery.

"Proud enough," he said, but there was no pride or anything else in his eyes when he added, "I was named after him. My uncle Carver. But I'm not a junior because he wasn't my father." We continued walking toward the Blue Demon, and when we got there, he opened the car door for me. I climbed in and thanked him.

But before I closed the door, he leaned forward. "My father said for you to call the lawyer, but will you call me before you do so I can talk to her? There's something I've got to get straight with her, something I've got to tell her before you tell anybody else. Please."

I knew then that he was much closer to Gabriella than he wanted to admit, so I took his card and stuck it into my wallet, thinking as I did that I had never seen such desperation in the eyes of a man so young.

3

By the time I worked the party nearly a week later, I'd forgotten the look in Carver Desmond's eyes, and by Saturday morning I could barely remember his face. Basil Dupre and his one-word warning were the only things on my mind. I'd turned around to fill somebody's glass, and he was gone. I desperately searched for him, wondering which door he slipped behind but it was as if he were in a dream. Truth was, the entire evening had a nightmarish quality to it: Amaretta and the story about the girl thrown off the roof. The sinister Delmundo Real. The tension that swelled inside me each time I poured a drink. It was as if Basil Dupre were an apparition, conjured up from some corner of my mind to ease it.

I left the party around three in the morning with

a brown envelope stuffed tight with fifty-dollar bills. The money had been slipped to me by a middle-aged white man who wouldn't look me in the eye but asked if I'd be available to tend bar again. I eagerly told him that I would. I had to find Amaretta and talk to her again. Although she hadn't admitted it, I sensed that she knew Gabriella Desmond. It wasn't so much what she'd said, but what she hadn't. If I worked again, chances are she would be there, and if I regained her trust, I could find some answers. But I would have to tread lightly; the mere mention of Gabriella had frightened her away.

I slept like a drunk when I finally dropped into bed and didn't open my eyes until ten. It was Saturday, and I made up my mind to enjoy it. I was in a reasonably comfortable hotel on somebody else's dollar, and despite my lack of success in finding Gabriella, I knew I should count my blessings. I slept for another half an hour and then got up and called my son, who was staying with my best friend, Annie.

I'd arranged for Jamal to stay there for the duration of my assignment, but his computer was at home so I'd given him permission to go there after school and on weekends. He still likes to play ball, but he also surfs the Net, which delights and occasionally concerns me. All in all, my son is a very good kid who reminds me constantly that he's *not* a kid and who made me promise I wouldn't call more than once a day while I was in Atlantic City. When I reached Annie, she told me he'd left earlier with some friends and, taking her cue from him, reminded me not to worry. "Jamal's a teenager, girl! It's truly time to let him grow up," she said with the confidence of a woman who has never raised a child. Nevertheless, I left a message on his pager to call me as soon as he got it.

After I hung up, I thought again about Dominique Desmond and what she had said about knowing Gabriella was in danger. I hoped her intuition was more reliable than mine, which works overtime most days and keeps me worrying about my boy far more than I should. I *always* want to know where he is going, what he is doing and who he is doing it with. If my child disappeared like her daughter had, I'd have to be put out of my misery. Except for when she had shown me her daughter's photograph, Dominique Desmond had been strangely detached, which was another thing about this case that was curious.

Around eleven, I showered, called room service for breakfast (the Desmonds could afford it, I decided) and sat at the narrow desk in the corner of the room to jot down some case notes on hotel stationery.

Cardell Cummings aka Rook. I put down his name first. Chances are the girl had run off with the boy even though her mother said it had been months since she'd seen her with him. But I'd sensed that the Desmonds' home was filled with secrets. How many did Gabriella Desmond keep? She was eighteen years old and probably determined to go her own way. What kind of boy was Rook? It would be easy enough to find out if he had a record, although it might be sealed. Where were his parents? As soon as I could, I'd call Jake and see if he could help me.

Amaretta. No last name. No place of residence. Just a little girl named after a drink. Where had *her* mama's intuition been buried? Had the woman ever cared? I share a bond with wounded young women; their sadness and vulnerability remind me of my own. My own mother's intuition hadn't kicked in very often, but my grandma's certainly had, and she'd had enough for both of them. If Amaretta had had a grandmother like mine, she wouldn't be on the street, I was sure of that. Something else worried me about Amaretta: the look that had been in her eyes before she'd gone into that room. Had I put her in danger?

Gabriel Wallace. I'd made an appointment with him through the Desmonds' lawyer shortly after I got into town for the first thing Monday morning.

He sounded pleasant and forthcoming on the phone, and I sensed that he knew more about his daughter's whereabouts than he'd told her mother. Children have an insatiable curiosity about blood kin, and despite Dominique's attempts to shield her daughter from her father, I was sure that Gabriella had been in touch with him. My own son's feeling toward my ex-husband—the intensity of his anger and his lingering sense of loss—have taught me how complicated and conflicted a child's feelings toward an absent father can be. Whatever the rest of the world thought of Gabriel Wallace, Gabriella shared his blood, genes and first name and that should not be easily forgotten.

And what about her family? All three family members—Dominique, Foster and even the stepbrother, Carver—had struck me as odd and secretive. Foster Desmond, especially, had rubbed me the wrong way. Could he be the reason his stepdaughter had run away? Dominique Desmond had set up the appointment and arranged it for a time when she knew her husband wouldn't be home. Had that been choice or chance? Desmond's attitude toward me as well as to his wife had been imperious and hostile. I suspected that he treated most women that way, including his stepdaughter. Men with attitudes like his usually feel that women are innately inferior and should be subjected to their superior will. Had he shown those feelings to his stepdaughter?

I'd been looking for Gabriella less than a week, and a clock was ticking. Serial killings are by definition random with no discernible motive, but what if the motives of this particular killer were simply not discernible to the police? Were there additional facts the authorities had decided to leave out of the press?

Go to the library! I jotted that reminder down and smiled as I did. Jamal had been after me for months to hone my computer skills so I could search for information online. Now I was forced to do my research the old-fashioned way. I needed to know more about the killings, and I would have to read through the lines of the news reports to get to the truth. I'd also need to find out more about teenage runaways, the Desmond family and Gabriel Wallace.

Layne Grimaldi. How close had she been to Gabriella Desmond? To Amaretta? The police were actively investigating her murder, and they'd be less than eager to share information with me, so I knew that anything I found would have to be on my own.

I finished my coffee, put my notes away and opened the heavy drapes. My room didn't offer much of a view, only the back edge of another casino and a sliver of beach, but the sun was shining brightly, beckoning me outside. I pulled on my jeans, a sweater and my sneakers and made my way downstairs.

I could hear the clink of the slot machines the moment I got off the elevator. It wasn't yet noon, but people of all ages were crowded into the casino. I'm not a gambler, but the lights and sounds were calling my name. I couldn't resist the chance to hit the jackpot, and I paused for a moment, taking it all in before I headed to the door that led to the boardwalk.

The chandeliers seemed brighter in the morning than they'd been at night, like swinging beacons, luring the weary traveler into a world of promised riches. My first night in town, I'd wandered into the casino in search of food and been drawn to a quarter slot machine called Wild Cherry. The name evoked the pleasant memory of the wild cherry cough drops I'd loved as a kid, and when I saw the name I could almost taste their tart flavor melting on the back of my tongue. Spurred by the memory, I'd dropped a quarter into the slot. To my surprise, fifteen dollars in shiny quarters had poured into the tray. It seemed like a treasure, and I felt a rush of happiness and excitement, as if I'd gotten away with something I shouldn't have.

Even now, five days later, I smiled as I recalled the experience. The cashier's line had been long that night, so I hadn't cashed in the quarters but poured the contents of the plastic cup into my bag. Each day I'd meant to empty it, but forgot until the weight and jingle reminded me, which was usually when I was already outside. I grabbed a white plastic cup now and scooped out handfuls of quarters, dropping them into the cup. An elderly man in a beige leisure suit, cigar clenched between his teeth, lazily fed quarters into the machine that had brought me luck. Disappointed, I took my place before a similar machine several feet down and eagerly shoved quarters into the slots, going for the jackpot.

The flashing bells and lights made me feel like a winner each time I pulled the lever. I was hypnotized by the clink of each coin as it dropped into the slot, and my breath stopped as I waited for the magical line of cherries or bars that would change my broke-ass existence forever. Each time the payline settled on cherries, my heart jumped, but then invariably pineapples, oranges or lemons would appear and disappointment surged through me. I knew that three quarters played at once would triple my winnings, so I shoveled them down in twos and threes—once, twice, a dozen times. I played my last seventy-five cents with hope and a prayer, and then stood in stunned silence when no change came out. Busted, I shook my Kenya bag, searching in vain for overlooked change. Then I remembered the twenty-dollar bill I keep stashed in the inner recesses of my wallet for emergencies. I pulled it out and desperately searched for the nearest cashier. It was then that I saw the woman, sent, I'm sure, by my grandmother, brother Johnny or some other long-gone soul who had and still has my best interest at heart.

She was slumped on a stool in front of a slot machine. Her body was stooped and crooked, and there was an overstuffed black plastic bag at her side. Her shabby jeans hung off her bony body, and her soiled gray T-shirt fit too snugly. Her hair fell loosely around her wrinkled cheeks, but the desperation that shone from her eyes was ageless. She glanced at me with a broken grin that seemed to wish me well. I returned her smile, but a shiver went through me. I shoved my twenty bucks back into my wallet and headed for the nearest exit.

Two giggling teenage boys about the age of my son edged into the casino as I left, then dashed away when an attendant scowled at them. A woman in her thirties cuddling an infant and holding a little girl's hand pushed past me into the building. The child paused at the door, her eyes wide as she gazed in wonder at the chandelier that shimmered above her. The mother yanked her impatiently, and the child followed her in, her eyes glued to the sparkling lights.

I stood outside and drew in a deep breath—a "cleansing" breath, my yoga-practicing friend Annie would call it—blew it out, then inhaled again, pulling in the smell and taste of the sea. Atlantic City had belonged to the ocean before it was bought by casinos, and that made me feel better about the city. As if to remind me of the city's origins, three gulls swooped down in front of me, screeching as they feasted on dirty onion rings and the seaweed that lay on the boardwalk. I walked past stores hawking Salt Water Taffy, Sea Foam Fudge and cheap all-you-can-eat meals. At the far end of the boardwalk, I could see the unlit lights that decorated the steel pier in the distance, and I stood for a while before I headed toward it and watched the ocean lap the edge of the beach.

I thought again about Amaretta. Had I made a mistake by keeping my identity to myself? If she was afraid, then I could find a way to protect her. I should have let her know there was somebody on her side, somebody she could depend on to fight a battle if she needed it. But she knew me as Tommie. She had no idea who I was or how to get in touch with me, and I felt guilty about that.

Stairs led to the beach from the boardwalk, and

I went down them to the beach, drawn by the roar and smell of the ocean. Slipping out of my sneakers, I walked along the edge of the water, carefully avoiding the sharp shells and bits of glass hidden in the sand. But the beach was cleaner than it looked from the boardwalk; the waves had pulled the debris away and the gulls swooped down to pick the sand clean.

I closed my eyes and pretended that I was back in Jamaica. The smell of the water was the same, so were the shells that gleamed in the sun. I picked one up, held it for a moment and thought about Solomon, my father's younger brother. When I was a kid, he had brought me shells back from Atlantic City: tiny ones, striped with brown and pink that brimmed over the top of a tin pail labeled with the city's name. He was dead now, killed in a car crash on his way back from here. Dead and gone like everybody else.

It was funny how quickly memories and names from this place rushed back: Chicken Bone Beach. The Boardwalk. Atlantic Avenue. Park Place. My parents giggling, sipping gin in the parlor against the wall of the tiny bedroom I shared with my siblings. Atlantic City—a magical city inspired, I thought, by Monopoly, my brother Johnny's favorite game. It was years before I realized it was the other way around.

How old was my young uncle when he died? Not more than twenty, I was sure of that. About the same age as me when I had my son. Two years younger than Carver Desmond. But there had been no sadness in my uncle's eyes. He was tall and handsome like my father had been before liquor stole his looks. They had been giants, my father and his brother. Their voices and presence always too big for the space they were forced to dwell in. Nothing could hurt or scare me when they were nearby. I haven't felt that safe since.

How long had my father wept for his kid brother? Was it weeks, months, years? I was certain now that it was the reason he started to drink. How could one careless moment lived by one carefree twenty-year-old change so many lives forever? His eyes had left the road for one second—thinking perhaps of the pretty girl he swore he would call or what he would tell his boss the next day or how he would tickle his young niece awake the next morning. Then he was gone, and his death would destroy my family.

I closed my eyes to erase my memories, then walked to the edge of the beach and tossed the shell as far into the ocean as I could throw it. The waves dragged it away to wherever they would take it, the same way they had taken Amaretta's kitten.

"You can never throw it far enough; sooner or later it will show up again," said a voice. I turned to face Basil Dupre. He was dressed in a tan cashmere V-neck sweater and well-tailored slacks, as casually elegant as ever. "I thought I might find you here, by the water." I continued my walk, and he kept in step.

"You recovered, then?" I asked after a moment. He looked puzzled, so I explained. "You were lying on a balcony in Jamaica in a pool of blood last time I saw you." He gave me a smile, which I returned because he always makes me smile even when I don't want to. I wish I could be less forthcoming, more coy, more in control of the situation, but I've never met a man who has such an effect on my judgment.

"Did you get my flowers?" He looked concerned and for a moment I thought about lying, demanding some answers: *No! I didn't get your damn flowers, and what do flowers mean anyway? Why didn't you let me know that you were okay? Why haven't I heard from you until now? How dare you assume that we can meet after so long and that nothing has changed!* But I knew that any questions I asked would receive no clear or easily defined answer. Basil takes the world and everything in it on his own terms or no terms at all. I knew that much about him. I wondered if I should let him back in my life, if I was making a dangerous mistake. But in the end all I said was, "Yes. I got them," and we walked in silence.

"The sea always brings me back to myself. Calms me down, like the touch of a pretty woman." He stole a quick glance, and despite myself I blushed, something I haven't done in a decade. "So tell me, Tamara, what were you doing there last night?" He was bringing things to the present, ignoring any hesitation I might have or questions I might ask, leaving the past where he thought it belonged. Each time we meet is a new encounter with no past or discernible future, just a present if I choose to live it. But I wasn't about to let him off that easily.

"Tell me first why *you* were there?" I tossed his question back at him, and he gave me an enigmatic smile that was no answer at all, so I answered him. "I'm looking for a young woman who ran away from home. I was working undercover last night, pretending to be something I wasn't."

"That is hard company you keep. Harder even than that club where I found you in Kingston. More dangerous. More violent." His voice was fearful, a quality I never thought I'd hear.

"Sometimes you've got to look for answers in dangerous, violent places," I said.

"So you've decided not to heed my warning?"

"One word, even from you, Basil, is not enough to make me back off from something I need to do. Don't you know me better than that?"

He gave a slight, hesitant smile. "Yes," he said. "I do."

There was a weatherworn bench near the stairs that led to the boardwalk and we sat down, barely touching. With the sun on my face, I closed my eyes, allowing myself to be seduced by the rhythm of the ocean, and for an instant it was as if we were back in Jamaica. But I've never been a woman who allows herself to be lost for too long in a moment.

"You didn't answer my question. Why are you here?" I searched his eyes for an answer.

"Then you're not glad to see me?" His voice teased me and a charming smile came to his lips.

"Tell me first, and then I'll tell you how glad or not glad I am to see you." I was serious and demanded an answer. His gaze dropped from mine but I saw a weariness in his eyes I'd never seen.

"I, too, am searching for a lost girl."

"I didn't know lost girls were your style, Basil."

"My style is whatever I need it to be," he gently corrected me. He was right about that. His style was his own.

Basil Dupre is a man with a past he doesn't talk

about and a future that rides the wind. He always has money but is vague about how he earns it. He protects his friends and haunts his enemies. He is a soldier of fortune who lives by his wits in a world of codes and ethics that I have never understood. But he is also a man of integrity who has saved my life on at least one occasion. I've always trusted my instincts about people and places, and I trust them when it comes to him. I know that he would never hurt me, but I'm also smart enough to know that when you get involved with a man like him you take nothing for granted. You take your chances, and often those chances aren't what you bargained for.

But I am a woman who has always taken chances. I took one when I became a cop and another when I left the force. I took one when I left my lying husband and chose to raise my son alone. I take chances each time I risk the well-being of myself and my child on my insight, guts and dumb luck. Basil Dupre is a chance that I've taken before. I wondered if I should take it again.

"How long has she been lost?" I asked him.

"For many years." I was puzzled by his answer, but instinct told me not to push him further. I knew he would say nothing if pressed, so we sat in silence as he decided if he wanted to go on, and when he did, his voice was haunted, as if recalling some dream or a distant memory. "When I was a boy, not much older than your son, I fell in love with a girl who left our town before we could marry. I tried to follow her but my father was murdered, and I did the things I had to do and went the ways I had to go. I left for the States. Came here. Lived my life and forgot about her except in my dreams."

"And she's the woman who is lost?"

"No. That woman died three weeks ago. She never left Jamaica and she lived much as she always had."

"But you loved her?"

"You never forget the first woman you make love to or wanted to marry, even though there are others who take her place in your heart. She married soon after she left me, had children. I wondered sometimes what had become of her but not enough to find her.

"A month ago in London, I ran into a friend from my parish, and he told me she was dying. He said it was good fortune that he saw me because she had begged him and others we knew to find me and tell me that she had to see me once more before she died. I had to be in Jamaica the next week, so I made it my business to visit her as she had asked."

"And she was dying?"

"Within the week she would be dead. Hard lives kill gentle women quickly there," he said bitterly. I thought of the gentle women I've known, and the toll hard times have taken. "But if I had known the whole story, I could—" He shook his head as if shaking off sorrow and continued. "She had wasted away to nothing. An old woman I would not have recognized if I'd seen her in the street, yet there was still a beauty about her. I could see how content I would have been if things had turned out differently. I could see how both of our lives would have unfolded. She would have been happier. I'm sure of that. She would never have died as unhappily as she did.

"Her first child and only daughter, was my child. She told me that before she died. She was pregnant before she left our town. Her husband, who was older than her and cruel even then, never accepted our child. He mistreated the girl and forbade the mother to contact me. She was a humble woman with no resources of her own so she did what she was told. The girl grew wild and free, an outcast who left home three years ago. She came to the States as I had, half-looking for me, I suppose, and she has disappeared. Her mother told me before she died. This lost child is the legacy of our love."

"What is your daughter's name?"

"Iris. The same as her mother."

"And you think you can find her in Atlantic City?"

"The last letter she wrote her mother was postmarked from here."

"How old is she?"

"Eighteen, if that."

"Do you know what she looks like?"

"I'll know her when I see her."

We sat there for a while longer until I asked him what I knew.

"And you think she is connected to Delmundo Real?"

He studied my face for a moment, kissed my lips, then left without answering me.

4

On Monday morning, as agreed, I went to visit
Gabriel Wallace. The narrow, worn streets leading
to his home reminded me of the ones I grew up
on, and the ancient buildings wedged between
proudly maintained single-family houses gave
me a feeling of déjà vu. He lived on the other side
of town, far from the high rollers and casino glitz.
His street looked like so many other ones in Jersey
cities—mom-and-pop stores that sell the basics to
those who don't have the means or wheels to go
anywhere else, torn basketball hoops tacked to
backboards in well-used backyards, little girls in
hair ribbons and jeans jumping double-dutch on
black-tar driveways. A place of families with high
hopes and dreams you can't kill. A street like the
one where I live.

Before I left the hotel I jotted down some questions in my notebook, but I wasn't sure what I'd get from Gabriel Wallace. I felt that stomach-churning nervousness I always feel before a crucial interview. Experience has taught me never to lead with the question I really want answered—the one that will get me thrown out. I work up to that one, get a sense of the situation and for the person I'm dealing with. Then if I'm asked to leave, I'll go with more than I came with. I had three important questions for Gabriel Wallace. The obvious one was if he knew where his daughter was. The second was if he knew anything about Rook aka Cardell Cummings. The one that would get me thrown out was if there was a possibility that Gabriella had become one of those "undesirables" he made his living abusing.

I rang the bell three times before it was answered by a large-boned white woman dressed in a plain gray dress. She introduced herself as Louella Wallace, Gabriel Wallace's wife, and I followed her through a shadowy hall into a dim living room, which was surprisingly dark considering the brightness of the morning. If I'd had any doubt that I was in Gabriel Wallace's home, this modest room set me straight. Religious and antiabortion signs and pamphlets were strewn everywhere. There were several enlarged grainy photographs of fetuses accompanied by large-print medical charts explaining abortion procedures in graphic detail. Crucifixes of every imaginable size, shape and color hung in every visible nook and cranny. A long banner with the words "Life to the Unborn" was unfurled across the fireplace. Stunned into silence, I sat down on the lumpy couch and piously folded my hands in my lap. Louella, noticing perhaps the look on my face, gave me a slight, sympathetic smile.

"It's a bit overwhelming, isn't it? My husband takes our political convictions very seriously."

"I can see that," I said, nodding in agreement and relieved that she seemed to have a sense of humor. We grinned at each other like girls for a moment, united in the way women sometimes are when they share their thoughts about the foibles of men.

"Are you a religious woman, Ms. Hayle?" She was still smiling, but the intensity of her stare broke our momentary bond.

"Yes, I am," I said because it's true; my grandmother saw to that. But I resented Louella Wallace's question, and my feelings showed in my face. A woman's beliefs are her own business.

"I mean to say, do you believe in life for the unborn?" She desperately searched my face for an answer.

"I believe in a choice for those who've already been born," I said, trying to make my voice sound reasonable and wondering if I'd be thrown out before I'd had a chance to warm the seat good.

"I believe that it is my responsibility to teach whenever I have an opportunity," she said, as if offering some kind of explanation as to why she was getting into my personal convictions. "I have led a life of sin. I have recovered. I was saved by a wise, brave man, and I will fight for the recovery of others." I wondered where all that had come from but nodded like I knew what she was talking about.

"And of course that wise, brave man was none other than the great Gabriel Wallace and the recovery of others is the life of the unborn?" I hoped she missed the note of sarcasm that crept into my voice.

"Yes." A beatific smile spread on her lips.

"I can't imagine you as a sinful person!" I said, my eyes wide with wonder and brimming with interest. If there's one thing I've learned in this business, it's to grab an opportunity when it comes, and this was one that couldn't be missed. I leaned forward, urging her on. It didn't take much urging.

"Gabriel will be down in a minute. He don't like me to dwell on the past." She glanced furtively toward the hallway.

"You can stop if you hear him coming. Sometimes the best way to teach is through example." I played the kindly advisor.

"I was a woman filled with sin," she confessed. "I was a lady of the night. A woman who sold her body." Her eyes turned cold for a moment as if she were thinking of something that made her angry. "Drawn into this by others. Led astray," she added.

"A lamb led to the slaughter by the evil that abides in these streets. May the slaughter always fall on the wicked." Gabriel Wallace's voice boomed from the hall as he entered the room. Louella and I shifted apart, confidantes no longer. I wondered how long he had been standing outside the door and how much he had heard.

Gabriel Wallace was as imposing in person as he appeared on television. He was close to six foot three and built like an athlete. I'd read somewhere he'd played football in high school; it wasn't hard to believe. He was a good-looking man, even though the muscles in his face seemed permanently fixed in a scowl. His fashion sense also left much to be desired. He was dressed all in white as usual. This morning it was an off-white polyester leisure suit with dark brown piping. A small gold cross studded with diamonds sparkled in his lapel, and a ruby ring with a cross embedded in it decorated the baby finger of his right hand. He sat down across from us in a large chair with a high back, taking on the look of a preacher about to hear the confessions of two wayward church members. He glanced briefly at his wife and then his gaze fastened on me, as if he could spot every evil secret I'd ever tucked away. I felt like a sinner.

"You spoke of your past life, but she didn't come to hear about the wages of sin and the lives of the incorrigible," he said to Louella, referring to me as if I weren't in the room. I also knew he was letting me know he'd heard what we said.

"But you can never tell how things will be connected," I said, defending Louella as well as myself, but then realizing that I probably should have kept my mouth shut.

"There is no connection between my wife's past and my child's disappearance."

"I'm sure you're right," I said, giving him his point even though I wasn't sure.

"My ex-wife's lawyer said you would be dropping by to discuss my daughter Gabriella. Exactly what can I help you with this morning, Ms. Hayle?" He gazed at me as if he were determined to be as cooperative and helpful as he could be. I reached into my bag for my notebook. He glanced at the notebook and then at me uncomfortably.

"No notes," he said, like somebody used to dealing with a hostile press. I tucked my notebook and pen back in my bag.

"First of all, I'd like to thank you so much for seeing me." I pulled out the old obsequious Tamara Hayle. "I'm sure with your help we'll be able to quickly find your daughter."

"If she's truly lost." Puzzled, I glanced at him but chose not to probe, at least not yet. I started with my first question, the most neutral and least likely to cause offense.

"Could you tell me when you last heard from her?"

"About three and a half weeks ago."

I stared at him with surprise but his expression didn't change. "Did you see her then or simply talk to her on the phone?"

"I saw her. She came by here."

I was sure he hadn't told Dominique Desmond, and I made a mental note to let her know. "Were you aware that she had run away?"

"The lawyer called me a couple of weeks after she disappeared, but this was the first time she'd been in touch with me."

"Did she say why she left?"

"She asked for my help," he said, sidestepping my question.

"Why did she need your help?" I asked, giving him room to maneuver.

"She is trying to save her life."

"Save her life?"

"Her life and her soul." He made it clear with his intonation that he had no intention of giving further clarification.

"Do you know where she is now?" I asked the most important question.

"No," he said emphatically.

"Has she ever mentioned a young man named Cardell Cummings? She may have called him Rook."

"No. Is that all you want?" He glanced once at his wife, then rose as if to leave.

"Could I ask a few more questions?" I was caught off-guard by his abrupt dismissal.

"All right." He settled down uneasily, never taking his eyes from my face.

"And last month was the first time you'd seen Gabriella in how long?"

"Seven years. As I'm sure you know, my former wife rarely let me see the child. My contact with her has been limited to phone calls and occasional visits."

"And you accepted this visitation arrangement?"

"You know how much money and power they have," he said, as if that explained it all. "Dominique Desmond is a very deceptive and extremely selfish woman, completely immoral. Her home is one of sin. She is as low as the whore of Babylon, she and that man she cohabits with." He spat out the words like some old-time prophet, as if it made him sick to say them. Louella nodded, enthusiastically agreeing.

"Does your daughter feel the same way?"

He paused, and then answered, his tone surprisingly reflective. "It wasn't what she said, but what was on her face, in her eyes. She was eleven when her mother stopped her from seeing me. The time when a girl needs her father most."

It was also the time when a girl coming into puberty might be scarred by the ravings of a fanatical father about female sexuality, contraception and sex. I had a renewed respect for Dominique Desmond's parenting instinct.

"But things speak for themself," he added, with a furtive glance at his wife, leaving me to figure out what he was referring to.

"You have very strong feelings about your former wife, would you mind elaborating?" A slow smile spread on his face, as if he were relishing the chance to set the record straight.

"My wife has always been a woman devoted to the buck," he said. For a moment, I thought he was making a cruel reference to Louella's former profession, but then I realized he'd simply forgotten to add the "ex." *Was it possible that he still considered Dominique Desmond his wife?*

"The first time she saw that man I knew she would leave me for him. She worked in his house, that big old house. Nothing but a maid, working for rich black folks instead of rich white ones. Man's wife wasn't dead for more than a year. Man was still in mourning, and in stepped my pretty Dominique, shaking her hips and batting her pretty eyes, and you know he was going through something deep, but not deep enough to ignore that long, pretty hair Dominique had hanging down her back."

I snuck a look at Louella to see if she had noticed this odd description of his former wife and her attributes, but she seemed not to have heard it. Or maybe she was used to it. Maybe he liked to put her down by elevating his ex-wife's charms. I lowered my voice slightly, out of respect for her even though she was sitting next to me on the couch.

"Were you still in love with Dominique when she left you?"

He looked at Louella this time as if asking her permission, then answered, "As in love as two kids struggling with a child but determined to make it could be. I didn't know nothing was wrong until she took up with him. It happened that fast." There was a glimmer of something in his eyes, and I realized it was pain, still there after all these years.

"So Dominique married him a year after his first wife died?"

"His first wife and his brother. Lost them both the same year. Dominique stepped right in with my sweet little daughter and gave him everything he thought he needed. And he did like them young, Foster Desmond did. Liked to snatch them young, just like they say the old man liked them."

"His older brother and his wife died close to each other?"

"The old man died first. Then the wife, I think her name was Dorothea. And there she sits now. The high-and-mighty Mrs. Dominique Desmond. But she ain't so high and mighty no more. What goes around comes around."

"And what has come around is the disappearance of her daughter," I said quietly, sensing that he knew more about his daughter's whereabouts than he was willing to say.

"I didn't say that," he said quickly. "What goes around is the suffering she is feeling, and the condition our daughter is in, and how she came to that condition, and what her coming to me means." The look of triumph on his face was puzzling.

"Meaning that your daughter is depressed and sad and angry at her mother," I said, filling in what I assumed he meant.

"Meaning my daughter is a sacred vessel, carrying the light of life," he corrected me, his eyes raised to the heavens. It took me a full minute to get the meaning of what he'd just said.

"Are you telling me that Gabriella is pregnant?"

"That's what I said." His voice was strangely proud for a father saying what he'd just told me, that his teenage daughter was pregnant.

"How pregnant is she?"

"Six months now. Too late for them to force anything on her, to make her do anything she doesn't want to do. She came to me, though. To me! She made her choice, and it was with me. With me." The lift of his head and the arrogance in his voice told me that that fact, more than anything else, excited him.

"Does her mother know?" I asked, but I was reasonably sure that she didn't. If she was six months pregnant now, then she'd been barely two when she'd left home in November. I'd known more than one teenager to hide a late pregnancy under bulky sweat suits and T-shirts and go on her merry way as if she didn't have a care in the world. It was clear to me now that she'd run away with Rook, whoever he was, who was surely the father of her baby. I suspected that they'd planned it together because they feared her family might try to force her to get an abortion that she didn't want to have.

"Did she tell you who the father is?"

"It is irrelevant," he said, which irritated the hell out of me, and then added, "Whoever it is, the child has the right to live. Whatever the father is, the child has the right to survive."

"I think the father might be a young man named Cardell Cummings."

"He's irrelevant."

"And you don't know where she can be found?" I asked again, no longer afraid to let him know that I suspected that he wasn't telling me the truth. "I have to inform you that if you know where she is and you are keeping that information from her custodial parents that kidnapping charges could be lodged against you." I knew that I was stretching the truth, and he gave it about as much credence as it deserved.

"The girl's eighteen. She can make her own choices. Go her own way."

"And she's out here by herself, pregnant, and maybe alone or dependent on a boy not much older than she is." My voice had risen and disgust with him was now reflected in my eyes.

"The Lord will provide."

"It doesn't worry you that there is a murderer loose in the city who is preying on young, vulnerable girls who are on their own and that your daughter could be the next victim?"

"The Lord will protect," he said, with a pious bow of his head. "Is that all I can do for you?" he added abruptly, and then he stood up, indicating that he was ready to leave.

"Yes," I snapped, truly irritated.

"Well, good day then," he said and left the room, leaving me and his wife sitting together on the couch as he'd found us. We listened to his footsteps as he ran up the stairs, then back down. I heard him clear his throat and the front door slam closed. Louella's body was tight, as if she were afraid to relax, but I sensed there might be more she had to say. I took my time digging around in my bag for nothing, hoping she'd tell me whatever was on her mind. Finally, I took the initiative.

"So how long have you been together?"

Her eyes grew troubled. "Do you mean how long have I been off the street?"

"No. I didn't mean that at all."

"Five years. Not long at all." She took a cigarette out of a side pocket of her dress and lit it with a quick glance at the hall. She inhaled the smoke greedily with that rush of enjoyment that smokers have with that first nicotine hit. I could still remember it, and she must have seen that look in my eyes. She offered me one, and I told her I'd quit a long time ago. She opened a window and then sprayed the room with air freshener. The scent of fake roses filled the air.

"Are you afraid of him?" I watched her closely as she answered. Although she was a big woman, I'd seen tiny men whip women twice their size nearly to death. I wondered if she would tell me the truth.

"I'm not afraid of too much of anything anymore," she said with a weary pride I admired. She took a long drag of her cigarette, then stubbed it out.

"It's one of the hardest habits there is to break. People who've done both say nicotine is harder to kick than heroin," I said, and she nodded in agreement.

"Used to do that, too. Heroin. Horse. Smack. Scag. That was how I ended up a whore. For a while it was crack, then it was crank, but now it's back to heroin. Any one of them can string you out quick, make you hard and mean. It was smack in my day, though. I kicked that, but you see I haven't kicked this one." She nodded toward the cigarette, acknowledging its hold over her, and I nodded, then smiled in agreement, hoping to establish a bond between us. One smoker to somebody who understood.

I was surprised by how forthcoming she seemed to be now, how much freer she turned in her husband's absence. But I'd seen that often with women married to men like Gabriel Wallace, who suck up all the air in a room. In that way, he was like Foster Desmond. Perhaps Dominique had married the same man with more money. Gabriel had described her as an aggressive gold-digger, but she may have cowered in his presence the same way she did in Foster Desmond's. Every story has two sides, and I hadn't heard hers.

"So your husband came into your life and everything changed for the better?" I asked Louella.

"I'm not on the street no more," she said, and I

nodded, acknowledging that she was right about that; better is always a relative term.

"What do you know about Gabriella?"

"Good girls can end up pregnant the same way they can end up on the block," she said, and she gave me a strange look that I wasn't sure how to interpret.

We sat there for a while in an odd, strained silence while I searched again for the nonexistent object in my bag. She smoked another cigarette, more relaxed this time. I took out a compact and spread some lipstick on my lips, and blotted it with a wrinkled Kleenex.

"Nice shade," she commented.

"Pathmark special."

"I thought P.I.s made big money."

"This one doesn't, but even if I did, at this point in my life, lipstick would be the last thing I'd spend my hard-earned money on," I said, and we both chuckled at my frugality and at hers, too, I assumed.

"Could I ask you something, Louella?" It was time to trade in on our momentary intimacy.

She hesitated, probably sensing what I was trying to do. "Yeah, but if I don't want to answer it, I won't."

"Louella, you strike me as the kind of woman a person in trouble could trust with a secret," I said and actually meant it.

"I can be."

"Do *you* know where she is?" I turned my attention completely on her now, placing my bag on the floor beside me. "Most good girls I know tell somebody they can trust where they're going, especially if they can't trust their mama or their daddy. They just don't go off into the night, at least in the condition she's in, without telling *somebody*. I think Gabriella might have told you more than you're saying. She obviously didn't tell her mother, and for reasons I'm sure you know, she didn't feel completely comfortable telling her father, but I'll bet she told you, didn't she? Has she ever mentioned Cardell Cummings to you?"

She was a woman who liked to keep secrets from her husband, hiding bits and pieces of herself from him and other people the way she hid the cigarettes. There was probably an occasional drink every now and again, quarters or dollars lost in the slots, clandestine visits to old friends still on the block. I leaned toward her, eager to hear what she had to say.

"About a week ago, she came by here right after that girl was killed. We talked awhile about it, and she gave me the address to a place where she said she was staying. It was impulse the way she gave it to me. Because she knew I cared about her. Slipped it to me before she left. Told me not to tell anybody, so I didn't."

"Is she living with Rook?"

"She didn't mention any boy."

Louella left the room and came back with an envelope with an address written on it, and handed it to me. "I'm giving this to you because you're a religious woman," she said.

"Thank you." I tried to sound as pious as I could. I quickly copied the address in my book and gave it back to her, thinking how secrets made this woman feel powerful and gave her the edge over her husband, and maybe even over his ex-wife.

She walked me to the door, then stepped out on the porch with me, almost as if she didn't want to say good-bye. I took advantage of her hesitation.

"Have you ever heard of a man named Delmundo Real?" I asked her.

She looked startled at the mention of his name. "He drops in and out of the scene. They used to say he was the devil." A chill went through me.

"I heard a young woman was thrown off a balcony in one of his suites."

"She probably deserved it," Louella said with a hatefulness that chased away any kind thoughts I'd had about her.

5

It was raining Tuesday morning, and that made me lazy; rain always does. I lay in bed for a while thinking about my son, and the skylight I remember needs fixing only when it rains. I wondered if I should call Jamal and tell him to stop by the house and put some newspapers under it before he headed to school but decided against it. He didn't need an excuse to be late. I'd deal with the leaky skylight and the mess it made when I got home.

I finally got up, ordered some breakfast (room service, of course, I was getting used to it). I had no idea what I would find when I went to the address Louella had given me, but I hoped it would make my life easier. I sure didn't feel like any crap on a dreary day like this.

Louella Wallace's crack about a murdered girl deserving her fate bothered me, but she'd given me what I needed, which is usually how it turns out: The hidden path always leads to the clearing. My favorite scenario was that I'd show up at the apartment, ring a doorbell conveniently marked *Desmond/Cummings* and find the young woman herself, eager to bring her pregnant self home to Mama. Or maybe the father-to-be—Cardell Cummings—would end up being young but earnest and hardworking and had swooped her away only because he knew the Desmonds would disapprove. Maybe he'd gotten a job in one of the casinos, was saving for college and everything would work out fine once they got a few years and bucks behind them. I ran through a half dozen other scenarios while I dressed, hoping that imagining a happy outcome would make it so. When I got downstairs, I called valet parking for the Blue Demon and followed a street map to the address.

I was surprised how close the apartment building was to the casinos, much closer to the heart of the city than the Wallace home, so close I was surprised I hadn't run into Gabriella on the boardwalk. The building, a stuccoed, four-storied structure painted a sickening shade of pink, was one of those once-elegant buildings that flourished in Atlantic City when the town had been a bonafide seaside resort, near enough to the beach and boardwalk to give it cachet. But hard times had battered its old-fashioned grace, and it looked like the last resort for jaded gamblers and con men down on their luck. The rain didn't help.

I dashed up the stairs to get out of it and searched in vain for Gabriella's name under one of the buzzers. I noticed what looked like a misspelling of the word "superintendent" scribbled under one bell and pressed it, hoping for the best. After a few minutes, it was answered by an elderly man in dungarees whose face and bald head had the patina of a new penny. He gazed at the rain for a moment in dismay, then at me and stepped aside with a grin.

"Well, I'll be damned! Guess that ad was right, huh."

"Ad?"

He kept grinning. "You know the one I'm talking about, the one you must have seen in the paper this morning, the one said: *Someone will come before day is done.* Newspaper's not even on the newsstand good, and here you are. Guess I got my money's worth." I had no idea what he was talking about, but I nodded in enthusiastic agreement anyway.

"Well, let me stop running my mouth and show

the thing to you. I got another one might be coming up, too, if you're interested. Two-bedroom. If them two young girls who are in it don't pay their rent, I'll be advertising for that one, too, and sooner rather than later. I'll show it to you while you're here and you can have first dibs if you want. Early bird gets the worm."

"Two young girls?" Maybe she wasn't with Rook after all.

"These kids' mouths are bigger than their stomachs these days. I lived with my mama till I was grown, then I moved in with my wife. Kids today fly from the nest before their wings can hold them good. I don't know what made them girls think they could afford a class place like this."

"I'd love to see both apartments, thank you." He was obviously a man who loved to talk, and I was eager to listen. I was also reasonably sure who one of those young girls was.

"By the way, my name is Jasper Johnston. But most folks call me J.J. for short. What did you say your name was?"

"Oh, ah, Tommie. Tommie Hayes."

"Tommie as in Thomasina? Now that's a beautiful name. My wife is called Nancy, but my dear mama was named Thomasina so I've always been partial to that name."

The horses were running my way.

"So how much money you want to spend on a place?" J. J. became the businessman.

"Depends on the place."

"Let me show you the one I advertised for first since that's probably the one you came to see. Then if them girls aren't home, I'll show you the other one." He ushered me into a foyer painted the same odd color as the building and gave the elevator button three hard presses. It creaked its way down to the lobby, and we got in.

"Needs some work," J. J. said with a disgusted nod toward the door as it slammed behind us. "Man supposed to be here this morning to look at it. I would have put that ad in tomorrow if I'd known somebody would answer fast as you did." He hit the second-floor button with his fist.

"How big did you say the second place is?" I casually tried to bring the conversation back to the apartment and its occupants.

"Two bedrooms. Real nice place."

"So you mentioned there were two girls living there now. Young people can be so hard on an apartment," I said, as if building maintenance were my main concern. "Can you tell me something about them and their lifestyle?"

"Between you and me, there's been all kind of kids going in and out of that place. Hard to keep track of them all. But things have cooled down some. This latest girl, the one who is in there now, is high-pregnant. If they don't get out soon, they'll be three."

"Pregnant? Isn't that a shame. And for a girl so young." It was time to start digging, and J. J. was handing out shovels.

"A young man comes around here every now and then. Far as I can tell, he ain't too much more than a boy, and he looked like he didn't belong to nobody if you know what I mean. But I ain't seen *grown* man the first come around here looking for anybody. At least not since the pregnant girl been in there. And what you expect? Women all over the television and movies having babies by themselves. Naturally young girls like that will do what they see in the movies. Like violence on TV. Then they wonder why kids pick up a gun and shoot somebody. Kids are kids. They don't know no better."

"They're lucky to have a landlord who cares about them." I can be shameless when it comes to flattery.

"Now don't get me wrong. It's not my business what my tenants do, or who visits them or any of that stuff, but these girls are young, and they are people of color, if you know what I mean. I guess that's what we call ourselves these days. We done gone from colored to Negro to black to minority to

African-American, and now we're back to colored." J.J. shook his head in exasperation.

"So both girls are African-American?" *Could one be Amaretta?*

"No. The pregnant one is black. The other one looks Puerto Rican."

"So how long have they been here?" I feigned casual interest.

"Well, the first one come in here about five months ago. Got the place from some man who looked Hispanic to me, too, but I ain't seen him since. That was a while ago. I guess the Puerto Rican is the one who's supposed to be paying the rent. The pregnant one has only been here a couple of weeks. Didn't bring too much with her but her belly."

We went through the first apartment quickly, and I nodded appreciatively as he pointed out its finer points. But I made it clear that I was really eager to see the two-bedroom, and we finally took the elevator down. J.J. rang the bell impatiently. Luck was still mine because nobody answered.

There was suddenly the possibility that I could end this case more quickly than I thought. When I verified that one of the young women was Gabriella Desmond, I would have found the missing daughter. My job would be finished. I could report my findings to the Desmond lawyer and leave it to her parents to decide how they wanted to handle it from there. I could go home to my son or maybe even take a short vacation down here—move to another hotel, have a massage and a facial, and if my luck was still holding, run into Basil Dupre. Now, *that* would be a treat. I was fantasizing about my next few days and calculating my daily expenses added to my fat check as J. J. opened the door and led me into the empty apartment.

As he'd described, it was a two-bedroom but a dismally small one, the room that served as a second bedroom hardly bigger than a large walk-in closet. The worn, institutional furniture had probably come with the place, and there was little else that looked like it belonged to the current tenants. No colorful posters taped to the walls. No photos of family members or best friends. No clothes carelessly dropped here or there. The traditional leavings of young people—magazines, CDs, paperback books—were nowhere to be found. It was a home for transients, custom-made for those who need to get up and out with no connections or complications.

The pager fastened to the pocket of J. J.'s shirt buzzed. He stared at it with annoyance, then turned it off.

"Must be the man who supposed to look at that

elevator. Let me go down and show him what he's got to do. You go on and look through the place and I'll come back up and get you as soon as I set things up with him," he said as he headed for the door.

"Thanks, so much," I said, not bothering to conceal the grin that spread on my face.

It would take me only a moment or two to verify if Gabriella lived here, and I began my search as soon as J.J. closed the door. I started with the small bedroom, assuming that the large one belonged to the woman who paid the rent. The best way to search a place is to start at one corner, usually the right, and methodically work your way across the room, turning up and examining everything your eyes and hands touch, looking in all the spaces near, underneath and in the way. There was a small chest of drawers in the far right corner and I started there, searching the drawers and running my fingers over and across its inside, where folks often tape cash or valuables. Then I moved to the small unmade bed, flipped the mattress up and searched underneath it and under the bed itself. But there was nothing—no magazines, paper bags, misplaced socks, nothing. The more I looked it became apparent that if Gabriella Desmond had ever lived here she had moved out, and if I'd had any doubt, her empty closet confirmed it. I sat on the bed for a moment, cursing to myself.

But the rest of the place was still worth a look. I went into the second bedroom that, thankfully, yielded more information. Clothes were neatly hung on satin hangers in the closet. Victoria Secret underwear, price tags still attached, were neatly folded in the drawers. Expensive shoes and sneakers were stacked against the wall. Several tubes of Chanel lipstick stood like sentinels on the bureau. I opened one, a deep, vampish red that suggested that its wearer was probably younger than she liked people to know and had dark hair and eyes. The clothes in this room were an eclectic mix of labels—Dolce & Gabbana and Prada thrown in with Gap and Old Navy. The king-size bed, far too large for the room, was topped with fancy throw pillows and embroidered sheets that looked like they had been snatched from a display ad for Bed Bath & Beyond. *Where did she get the money for fancy sheets if she couldn't pay the rent?*

A tattered rag doll with knit braids and red dots for cheeks leaned against one of the pillows. It brought a smile to my lips because it made me remember the stuffed green snake my brother Johnny bought for Jamal when he was a boy. I'd recently found it in a corner of his closet as torn and probably as loved as it had been when he slept with it every night. Caught up in my memories, I picked up the toy, hugged it, then placed it back where it had been. With all her lipstick and lace undies, the young woman who lived here was nothing but a kid at heart.

The bathroom was next, and the cabinet over the sink was a treasure trove of secrets. A bottle of prenatal vitamins prescribed to G. Desmond at this address confirmed Gabriella's presence, so she'd probably left in a hurry. If she was conscientious enough to get a prescription for vitamins in the first place, she would make it her business to get some more. I scribbled down the name of the drugstore, the obstetrician, and the prescription number with the intention of calling them later to find out what I could. The name Jayne Lucindo was printed on a prescription label for Valium and birth control pills, which sat next to a pack of condoms. At least Ms. Lucindo, whoever she was, believed in protecting herself. Variously shaped bottles of facial lotion, old makeup, tubes of mascara, hair pins and hair elastics lay in a careless jumble on shelves. I picked up a bottle of prescribed lotion and looked for a name. The door slammed. I put the lotion down. "Mr. Johnston, I'm in here," I yelled out, making my voice as cool and collected as I could.

There was silence and then a frightened voice. "Who's there?"

I closed the cabinet door, turned on the faucet,

let it run for a few moments and then turned it back off. I walked into the living room bold as could be, but wearing a sheepish, friendly grin.

"I'm sorry to have frightened you, miss," I said pleasantly, extending a hand. The young woman stared at me as if I'd handed her a rat. "I thought you were Mr. Johnston. He let me in and told me I could look around. I was in the bathroom testing the water pressure. You can never tell with these old apartments."

Jayne Lucindo was a stunningly pretty girl with thick black hair that flowed halfway down her back. Her eyes, nearly the same dark color as her hair and fringed with thick lashes, were wide with curiosity. She looked about eighteen, if that. Her jeans and a tight-fitting red T-shirt were covered by a yellow parka that was wet and which she tore off and dumped into a nearby chair as I spoke. The gold hoops in her ears were almost as big as bracelets. She slammed the shopping bag down on the table; it rocked from its weight.

"Damn that old man," she muttered. "He can't even wait for me to get out of here good before he goes and shows this damn place to somebody else. I can't stand that old man."

"I'm sorry. I really assumed you knew I was coming," I said, hoping J.J. would stay gone awhile longer.

"How does he know I'm not going to come up with the rent?" She glared at me and then began to unpack the grocery bag, shoving a jar of Jif peanut butter and a bag of Oreo cookies on a shelf. She opened the refrigerator and placed in cartons of orange juice and milk, which, save a bottle of *Sprite*, was empty. "He don't know nothing about me. I'm sick of this damn place anyway." She snatched the soda from the refrigerator, poured herself a glass and then turned to me. "Want some?"

Under the circumstances, her hospitality surprised me. "Thank you very much," I said. She poured me a glass, and I sat down across from her at the wobbly kitchen table.

"Listen, I didn't mean to alarm you," I apologized again.

She shrugged. "It's not your fault. It's that dumb old man's fault for letting you in in the first place."

"It's a great apartment."

"It's a crummy little shithole and I hate it." She took a gulp of soda.

I took a gulp of mine. "Do you live here by yourself?"

"You been through the place, don't you know?" She leaned back in her chair and eyed me skeptically. I avoided her stare.

If I told her the truth, I'd have to admit to her, and later to J.J., that I'd entered her place under false pretenses, which would be embarrassing and possibly illegal. It might also make her angry and suspicious enough not to share anything she knew about Gabriella's whereabouts. But if I told her who I was and she did know where Gabriella's was and wanted to get in touch with me later, she'd be able to do it. On the other hand, if I stuck to my story, I might be able to pull out more information. At least now I knew that Gabriella had been here and gone, which was more than I knew yesterday. But maybe Jayne Lucindo knew still more and could point me, albeit unwittingly, in another direction. I decided to play it both ways and go with the truth only if it became necessary.

"My roommate skipped out on me." She decided to answer my question. "She was supposed to help with the rent, but she didn't give me nothing. So you want to wait around here until he comes back?" She began putting groceries into the cupboard: a box of Ritz crackers to go with the peanut butter. A jar of Vlasic dill pickles. Six bags of grape Kool-Aid. A half pound of sugar. Paul Newman popcorn. Nothing life-sustaining. No vegetables or fruit. Teenage junk food.

"You sure you don't mind?"

"No, go ahead. You're here now."

I went into the living room and looked around.

"So you live around here?" She called out from the kitchen. There was a hint of suspicion in her voice. When she thought my back was turned, she sneaked a look, regarding me warily.

"For the time being, I'm staying in a hotel. The Sultan's Lair." The putting away of groceries stopped; there was dead silence. "Do you know the place?"

"So you work there?" She began moving things around on the shelf.

"On and off."

"What do you do there?"

"I tended bar a couple of days ago. Private party. Big penthouse suite. Big-time players." I glanced in her direction; her back had stiffened. I came back into the kitchen and sat down at the table.

"So you're saying J.J. let you in here and you came to check out my place?" She stared at me doubtfully, daring me to tell her a lie so I knew I had to go with the truth or "get the hell out" would be her next words. I thought about Amaretta and my regret about not having been honest with her.

"No. Ms. Lucindo. I didn't come to look at your apartment even though that's what I told your superintendent. My name is Tamara Hayle. I'm a private investigator, and I was hired to find Gabriella Desmond. I came to talk to you about her." Her eyes grew bigger now than when I'd mentioned the Sultan's Lair, and she sat back down across from me. "I was told by a source that Gabriella was living here, and that is why I came to see you."

"You're a private investigator?"

"Yes."

"Who told you Gabriella was here?" Her eyes were no longer suspicious but afraid, and that was puzzling.

"I'm not at liberty to say."

"Who hired you?"

"I'm not at liberty to say that, either."

"Get the hell out of my house." She said it anyway.

"Listen to me for a moment." I spoke firmly, using the same patient but authoritative tone I use with my son, and it worked on her in the same way, which told me something, too—about her past and that somebody had once cared enough about her to exercise that kind of control over her life. "Okay. You have a right to be suspicious. You should be. It shows you have street smarts, and that's a good thing to have in a place like this but I'm on your side. I don't mean you or Gabriella any harm. In fact, I will give you the names of a police captain in Belvington Heights and two lawyers in Essex County, which is where I live, who will vouch for me and tell you I'm on the level. You'll also be paid for any information you give me. But first you have to tell me why you are so afraid."

"No reason," she said too forcefully.

The door opened, and we both jumped. J.J. glanced around cautiously, rolled his eyes and stepped into the apartment. "I thought you were out for the day," he said, somewhat apologetically to Jayne Lucindo.

"How do you know I'm not going to come up with the rent?" Jayne snapped, ignoring his apology.

"'Cause you ain't come up with it yet and it's almost April," J.J. snapped back.

"It's only a month late." Jayne's voice dropped a decibel and her eyes begged for understanding. J.J. was firm.

"I got a right to show this place when you're late two months in a row." Softening his voice, he turned to me. "Have you seen what you wanted to see?" I glanced at Jayne, waiting for her reply, her permission for me to stay.

She kept me on hooks for a minute and then said, "She's going to look around a little more. I came in before she was finished."

"Ain't that much to see." J.J. looked perplexed.

"I'm going to tell her what it's *really* like, living

in this dump with a nose-always-in-your-shit superintendent," Jayne threatened, her voice louder
now, her mouth in a pout.

"Talk to me like that, and you'll be out of here
on your fast little butt before you can say howdy-
do." J.J. pouted now, too. "When you're finished,
Ms. Hayes, come on down to my place, and we
can talk some more. I'm in the basement." He
threw Jayne another dirty look and slammed the
door behind him.

"Tell me the names," Jayne said as soon as the
door was closed. I wrote down the names of my
lawyer-friend Jake Richards, and Captain Roscoe
DeLorca, whom I used to work for in Belvington
Heights, and gave her one of Sam Henderson's
cream-colored, engraved business cards. She
went into her room and came back in about fifteen
minutes.

"The lawyer on the card said you'd pay me
right away. A thousand dollars. He said you'd pay
me today if I want."

"I'll go to an ATM and get the money whenever
you want me to get it." She looked impressed and
then doubtful.

"Even if I don't tell you much? I don't know
that much."

"Anything you say is enough for the money."
I've always liked playing Robin Hood.

"The lawyer on the card said on his word as an officer of the court that he represented the person who hired you and she won't do anything to harm Gabriella. I don't trust lawyers. Can I trust him?"

"You can trust this one," I said. "Now tell me where she is."

She looked lost for a moment and helpless when she answered. "I don't know where she went. I got home from work night before last, and she was gone. There was no note, nothing. She just took all her shit and was gone."

"How long had she been living here?"

"Just a couple of weeks."

"Why did she move in?"

"Because she needed somewhere to go."

"Where was she living before?" I asked, even though I knew.

She avoided my eyes. "With another friend. She had to leave. Get out fast 'cause she was scared."

"Scared of what?"

"Of being killed like our friend was."

"Layne Grimaldi?"

"Yes."

"You said you were at work when Gabriella moved out. Where do you work?"

"For a guy who hangs out in the casinos." Her gaze fell to the floor as she spoke. I thought about mentioning Amaretta and Delmundo Real but then decided to wait. I didn't want to push too much too fast and chase her away the way I had Amaretta. Instinct told me to keep it on Gabriella for a while.

"And you don't know where to find her?" Her hesitation told me she did.

"If I knew I'd tell you. I really don't know. She left fast. Too fast."

"When did you meet her?" I changed directions.

"A couple of months ago. On the boardwalk. She was a friend of my best friend's." Her eyes watered.

"Was your best friend Layne Grimaldi, the girl who was killed here Friday before last?"

"Yes," she said in a small voice and began to cry.

I've been through enough grief in my life to know how to offer some comfort, and this girl obviously needed it. I held her hand in mine, and she took it cautiously, then held on for dear life, like a scared kid grabbing the hand of somebody else's mother.

"I haven't talked to anybody about Layne, not even the cops," she said after a moment.

"Maybe it's time you did."

"No."

"Why not?"

"Because there's nothing I can do about it. She was just killed, that's all."

"Why don't you try," I said. "Just say it out loud. Let it out, and tell me what you can about her." She gazed at my face for a moment, wondering if she could trust me, and then let go of my hand and went into the bathroom. She came back with a roll of toilet paper, cried for a while longer. When she spoke, her voice was hoarse.

"We got to be friends because our names sounded alike," she said, a smile now on her lips. I thought again how young she was, far younger than she looked. "Jayne and Layne. We even spelled it the same way. We really looked alike, too, even though she was white. We had the same coloring and hair and everything. We used to tell people we were sisters. We kind of hung out together. Neither of us had anybody else." Sorrow came into her eyes again.

"Did Layne live by herself?"

"Yeah. She had money left over from her mother's insurance policy, and her daddy died when she was little. She did some drugs for a while but she cleaned herself up. By the time we met, she'd gone through a lot of the money, but she still had enough to afford the place where she lived, so she lived on her own, and then I moved in to help with the rent until I could find a job and get my own place. Then a couple of other girls moved in with me, and Gabriella moved in and then it happened. Then Layne got killed."

"And you think it was the man, the serial murderer that everybody is talking about?"

"I guess so," she said with such hesitation I wondered what else she knew.

"What do you mean?"

"I guess it was him," she said more firmly this time.

"What kind of drugs did Layne do?" I wondered if her dabbling had led her to her killer. That could be the link between him and the other women who had been murdered. And maybe even Gabriella.

"Anything she could get. I know that," she added.

"Do you know why she settled in Atlantic City in the first place?" I was wondering why Jayne was here, too. Atlantic City seemed an improbable place for young women to move to. Not like New York City or some of the other big cities. Her smile disappeared as quickly as the first one had.

"Same reason as me. Her mother used to bring her to the beach here when she was a kid. She had memories about the boardwalk and the ocean and she wanted to live here because of what she remembered."

I thought about my shells and the laughter in my parents' kitchen and the way my young uncle's soft beard touched my cheek when he kissed me. Memory was as good a reason as any to move to a place like this.

"What about you, Jayne? Where are your people?"

"My mama's dead. She loved me very much but she's dead now, and my daddy walked out when I was a kid because he didn't get along with my mama, and I don't know where he is, and I don't care anymore," she added with a studied toss of her head that was supposed to look careless but didn't. "Do you have any kids?"

"Yeah, I do," I said.

"A daughter?" she asked, and I knew she was thinking about her own mother.

"No. A son."

"Where does he live?"

"Where I do. Tell me more about Layne."

If she noticed my hesitancy to reveal more about myself, she didn't show it. "So me and Layne started hanging out, doing things together, going to the same clubs and parties. Meeting people, going on dates, making money, doing shit. Then Gabriella popped up on the boardwalk one day with this guy we know named Rook. She wasn't showing yet, and we all started hanging out together. Remember that TV show 'Josie and the Pussycats'? It was like we were Josie and the Pussycats." She hummed the theme song playfully, which I hadn't heard since Jamal was a baby.

"But weren't there four Pussycats?"

"Then Layne got herself killed and Gabriella shows up here, and she's scared and I let her stay for a while," she said without answering me. "Gabriella said she would help me get some money. She said she knew how to get a lot of money quick, and then she disappeared."

"Tell me about Gabriella."

"Gabriella is weird, man. Like she won't tell you nothing about herself. She's real secretive. She spaces out, though. Like she bumps into shit a lot, like she doesn't know her own body, even though she's pregnant. She's kind of otherworldy, if you know what I mean."

"Otherworldly?"

"Like her mind's on something else. The only other thing she thinks about is Rook."

Finally.

"Do you know him?"

"Who, Rook? I seen him around."

"Why do they call him Rook?"

"Because he likes to play chess, and he says that's his favorite piece. He used to hustle chess when he lived in New York City."

"Does he still live there?"

"No. He lives here."

"What kind of guy is he?"

"Just a guy, that's all."

"How old is he?"

"Seventeen, eighteen. I don't know."

"Where are his people?"

She laughed bitterly. "The same place as everybody else's."

"So he doesn't have family. Is he a runaway?"

"If that's what you want to call him."

"Where does he live?"

"Hell if I know."

"What does he do?"

"Take care of Gabriella," she said with a little smile.

"Is he the father of her baby?"

"Ask her when you see her," she said with an insolent toss of her head.

"Where can I find him?"

"I thought you were asking about Gabriella. I don't tell nobody else's business, okay. That will be extra money, for Rook." She said it angrily, and I took the hint.

"Tell me some more about Gabriella, then."

"Gabriella? She could be like Miss Goody Two-Shoes when she was in the mood. She didn't like to talk about sex and shit like that. She could act like the Virgin Mary sometimes around here. Like that baby she carried in her belly was like an immaculate conception or something. Sometimes she could freak out, too, like she was crazy. Start screaming over nothing. Very weird. The only one who can calm her down when she gets crazy like that is Rook."

"You don't sound like you liked her much."

"Well enough. We all kind of looked out for her. Like she needed to be protected. We felt sorry for her. But I would have felt something else if I'd known she was going to skip out and leave me with the damn rent. All because—" She paused and shook her head as if reminding herself of something. "All because she felt like it, I guess. Spoiled little rich girl always gets her way."

"So Gabriella told you about her family?"

"No."

"How do you know she's rich?"

"She *looks* rich. Dresses rich. I can look at a chick and tell if she's got cash by the shoes she wears," she said with a glance down at mine, which revealed the sorry state of my finances.

"So these dates you went on with Layne, what was that about?" I switched gears from my shoes back to Layne. I didn't mean my tone to sound judgmental, but I could tell by the look on the girl's face that it did. Her voice rose a few notches when she answered.

"We weren't doing men for money, if that's what you're talking about and I can tell by the look in your eyes that's what you meant. That's not what we were about. Me and Layne weren't, anyway. But if they gave us some we'd take it. Know what I mean? Gabriella was pregnant and the Virgin Mary so you know she wasn't doing nothing. So you can give that up right now."

"That wasn't what I meant." I tried to explain even though it was exactly what I meant. But I had to admire Jayne's spunk. She was serious about defending her honor and that of her dead friend. "I asked about the dates because that might be important to where Gabriella has gone."

"She's probably with Rook somewhere."

"Then where is he?" I went back to that.

"That's your job, not mine."

"So Gabriella didn't mention her family?" I tried that again.

"No. She didn't talk much about herself. Are they the ones who are looking for her?" I wondered again how much she knew.

"If they were, would it matter?"

She shrugged again, her deliberately nonchalant shrug. "No."

"So all of you were on your own and you got by the best way you could?" I backtracked.

"Most of the time. Sometimes we had to borrow money."

"Who did you borrow from?"

"People we knew," she said, shifting her gaze

again. "So is that enough to get my money?" she asked, telling me the interview was over.

"Two more. Then we can go and get it," I said. "If you have people who you can borrow from, how come you're so eager to get it from me?"

"My money source turned dry," she said with a short, bitter laugh.

"Do you know a girl named Amaretta or a man named Delmundo Real?"

She wasn't tough enough to hide the dread that widened her eyes and made the corner of her mouth droop for a second. But she was hard enough to look me in the eye and lie. "No," she said. "And that's three. Can we get my money now?"

So we drove to the casinos where she said we would find the closest ATM and walked into the Sultan's Lair together. I asked a few more questions, but she'd said all she was going to say. I got her money in crisp hundred-dollar bills from several ATM machines, and she stuffed the cash into her tiny black Coach bag without looking at or counting it. I asked her if she wanted me to drive her home again, and she said she'd take a cab.

We were walking toward the cabs in the back of the hotel when Carver Desmond pushed ahead of us on his way into the casino. He didn't see me at first. His face was tense, and he stared straight ahead. He turned and grinned when he caught my eye, giving Jayne Lucindo that quick, appreciative once-over that men give a pretty girl. Jayne returned his gaze, her well-trained eyes probably taking in his expensive clothes—his herringbone tweed pants, silk T-shirt, micro-suede brown shirt, Rolex watch. But they didn't speak, and she left through the swinging doors of the hotel with a seductive swing of her hips.

"Does she know my stepsister?" Carver asked. There was such concern in his voice that after hesitating a moment, I told him what I knew.

"Where is Gaby?"

"I don't know yet," I said.

He turned his gaze on me, his eyes boring into mine. "Have you found out anything else? You promised me you would tell me. Please." His voice was anxious, even more desperate than it had been before. "What about him? That stupid nigger who was sniffing around her?"

I recoiled again. It was the way he said the word, like a white man would say it.

"I've heard a few things, but nothing definite. I'll let you and your parents know when I hear anything definite, don't worry." We walked toward the gaming room. "So you're down here visiting people or just coming to the city?"

"I come down to play the slots, sometimes.

Cards, that's all. My dad comes, too, sometimes. No big thing," he said.

"Did your father come down with you this time?"

"Yeah, but he just stayed a day or two. Then he left to go back home. He had some business to take care of." I wondered if Foster Desmond had decided to check up on me.

"Did he stay at the Sultan's Lair?"

"Here? Yeah, for a night. Then he went to my aunt's old place. Do you like to play?"

"No. I don't gamble."

"Not even on a sure thing?"

"There are no sure things."

"You don't think so?" He gave me the same shy, slow smile he'd given me when we met and hurried into the casino. I knew then what it was that drew him.

6

The arrival of the roses on Saturday morning came at the same time as the call. I didn't make the connection at first, although any fool with a working brain should have made it. I wondered later if I was losing my touch, neglecting the God-given intuition my grandma so generously bestowed that has saved me from tripping over my big feet more times than I can say. In the long run it probably wouldn't have mattered much one way or the other. I know one thing though: roses will never smell the same.

I was tired by Saturday and frustrated by my lack of progress. In the days following my meeting with Jayne, I strolled down the boardwalk so many times folks were beginning to look at me funny. I snacked on salty fries and greasy burgers in every fast-food joint within walking distance. I lost about a hundred bucks at gambling tables in other casinos. I nursed weak drinks in lousy bars and fought off drunks in the mob-run clubs up and down Georgia and Pacific. And still I turned up nothing.

The women at Covenant House were kindhearted and helpful but there was nothing new they could tell me. It was as if Gabriella Desmond, Rook and Amaretta had dropped off the edge of the earth. Several days after visiting her, I'd parked in a secluded spot outside Jayne Lucindo's apartment building, waiting and hoping to see her, Gabriella or the boy coming into or leaving the apartment. But nobody came or went.

I rang J.J.'s bell one day in frustration, confessed my true identity and begged him not to slam the door in my face. After shaking his head in disgust, he told me what he knew because he was a "sucker for a mama and her lost baby." After he'd left Jayne with me that Tuesday, she returned later that night and gave him four hundred dollars in twenties. She promised him the rest of the two thousand dollars she owed him a week later. That was all he knew, he said. I thanked him, gave him my card and asked him to call if he saw either her, Gabriella or the young man whom he mentioned before.

The roses came the next morning.

"Ms. Tamara Hayle?" the bellman asked, handing me an oblong white cardboard box tied up with a fancy black lace ribbon. I tore it open and gasped in pleasure at the bouquet of long-stemmed red roses peeking from the green and white tissue paper.

"Well, I guess you done rocked somebody's boat!" the bellman observed with a snicker as I reached into my wallet for his tip. It wasn't hard to guess whose boat I'd rocked. The delicate scent of the flowers filled the room, and I smiled at the thought of Basil Dupre, the only person in town who knew my real name and where I was staying. It was a long time since a man had sent me flowers—longer than I liked to remember. The phone rang, and assuming it was Basil I answered it with a grin on my face.

"Hello?" I chirped into the phone.

"I am calling for Delmundo Real." The man's voice was heavily accented and deep with a malevolence that made me stiffen. "Delmundo Real has requested that I call you. He would like to see you, to talk to you as soon as possible. Right away. About a job."

English wasn't his native language, and he stumbled over the words, hesitating over "job" long enough to make me wonder if he was talking about more than the word implied. A line of sweat snaked its way down my back.

"Job? For when? Tonight?" I tried to sound casually unconcerned.

"We talk when you get here."

"You want me to come now?" I tried not to let my apprehension seep into my voice.

"Now. We talk when you get here. Now." Was he from Eastern Europe? Russia? I knew the Russian mob had gained a foothold in South Jersey along with Miami and the Caribbean. Had they connected with Delmundo Real? I tried to recall the face of the man who had given me the money last Saturday, but it had been so late and I'd been so tired, I could scarcely remember anything about him.

"Why do I have to come now? You either want me to work tonight or not." I dropped the casual tone and made my voice sound hard—the tough Tamara Hayle I trot out when I need her.

"A few things we got to get straight . . . Mr. Real got to get straight. Please come now." He hung up. I was sure that "Mr. Real" had been standing nearby listening to every word.

It was time to pay the piper for the room service every morning and the expense money deposited daily into my bank account. If I was going to find Gabriella Desmond I would probably have to find

Amaretta and checking out Delmundo Real was one of the things I'd have to do. Amaretta was an important lead, and the last time I'd seen her she had been with Real. This was part of the the job I had been hired to do and if it meant stumbling into "dangerous, violent places" then I would have to stumble. A shiver went through me. I chased it away. It was broad daylight, I reminded myself. People don't get thrown off balconies in broad daylight. Or do they?

I went through the few clothes in my closet and settled on a pants suit loose enough to move around in with pockets deep enough to conceal a small canister of pepper spray and a Swiss army knife with a sharp blade. If somebody frisked me, I could explain them easily. A girl needs protection in a city like this, with all this killing going on, I would say, with a girlish bat of my eyes, something I can still do with effort. I doubted these "weapons" would be much help, but I didn't want to go with no protection at all.

I took the elevator to the thirty-third floor and then boarded the private elevator to the penthouse. It was one of the more stressful rides of my life. I took a couple of deep breaths before the elevator door opened and I got out. Assuming that I was being watched by a hidden security camera, I struck a casual pose while I waited. I felt the weight of the Swiss army knife in my pocket and felt better. I took out my compact and a tube of lipstick and spread some on my lips. I pasted a smile on my face. My hands were shaking. I made them stop. I pressed the doorbell, and the door opened before the bell rang. A heavyset man stood in front of me, his hands hung at his sides. With no greeting or expression on his face, he nodded for me to follow him into the penthouse, which I did without comment or hesitation.

The place reeked of marijuana and men's cologne. It looked different in daylight: The off-white walls were smudged with fingerprints, and the sunlight that streamed in through the enormous windows dulled the shine on the cheap gold-leaf trim and called attention to the shabby velvet fabric on the couches. Although the doors to the bedroom were closed, I could hear laughter and loud voices coming from behind them. The gaming tables that took up so much of the space when I'd been here before had been replaced by a black marble table. Empty beer bottles and an open bottle of gin stood amid piles of magazines and *Racing Forms*. A cigar had recently been snuffed out on its surface, and the odor mingling with the other smells in the room made my stomach turn. The glass doors that led to the balcony were open. I thought about Amaretta. The man's eyes followed my gaze.

"You wanna go out there and wait?" he asked. Startled, and unsure how to answer, I stared for the first time at his dull face. He wasn't the man from the other night, the one who had paid me and spoken to me on the phone that morning. His face was ruddy, and his dark blond hair was thinning. His eyes were empty of expression and told me nothing. He could have been a storekeeper from my old neighborhood or maybe a butcher or even a cop. He was dressed in a dark suit that looked like it had been bought for somebody else. I forced Amaretta and the girl from the balcony out of my mind and forced myself to walk to the open doors and step outside with an attitude. Dared myself to do it.

The sunlight and breeze made me feel as if I'd stepped into another world, and I took a breath and relaxed. The balcony was longer and wider than it appeared from inside, and more tastefully done than the suite. Large clay urns filled with miniature trees sat near the railing and a small black iron table surrounded by four chairs stood in the center. I could see the beach and ocean from where I stood as well as the adjoining wings of the hotel. Impulsively, I counted down twenty stories in the direction of my own room, but all the windows looked alike, the heavy draperies closed or partially drawn. Hypnotized by the waves, I watched the ocean for a while longer and then stepped back into the living room, closing the terrace door behind me. The room was empty, and I sat down on the couch. Impulsively, I picked up one of the magazines, then threw it down in disgust when I realized it was pornographic.

The doorbell rang, two very long rings, then a short one, as if it were a signal, and it was quickly answered by the man who had let me in. I couldn't see who the guests were, but I listened hard, wondering if one was Amaretta. As they came in the direction of the living room, I stood and peeked around the corner and was just able to catch a glimpse of a woman. She was pretty with a haunting face, shaped like an oval with full lips, high cheekbones and skin the color of coffee. And she was very young, I could tell that much in a glance. I thought about Basil Dupre and some instinct told me it might be his daughter. I moved toward the door, not sure what I would say or do but knowing I should make some attempt to talk to her. But someone grabbed my arm above the elbow and held it very tight, squeezing until it hurt. The thick shag carpet had concealed his footsteps.

"But you have just arrived," said Delmundo Real. He held me with the grip of a man who expects to get his way without asking for it. I tried to snatch away, but he held me tight, letting me know that he was stronger than I. Finally, he released me.

His eyes were cold, as I expected they would be, but they also had a savage glint. He nodded toward the couch. I sat down, and he sat in a chair across from me. His eyes rested for a moment on the cover of the magazine I'd put down and then his gaze returned to me. He crossed his legs, as slowly and seductively as a woman. His feet were bare, and his toenails were polished and buffed, as if he'd just gotten a pedicure.

Taken independently, each feature on his face would have been that of an exceptionally handsome man. Together they were exotic but unsettling. The stubble of his beard on his pointed chin emphasized his flawless skin and the angular shape of his face. The ponytail of a week ago was gone, and his black hair flew loose around his chin in a cloud of silky swirls. He smiled a smile that wasn't one, and I noticed his perfect teeth, as pearly and even as if they'd been cut from ivory. His long, gaunt body was wrapped in a black velour robe as lush as cashmere.

"I like to know the girls who work for me. It gives me a personal sense about them. In the kind of business I'm in, it makes things easier for everybody, don't you agree?" I was struck by the low, melodious sound of his voice. It had a seductive lilt to it, a bewitching quality that made you want to hear it again. I couldn't place the accent, whether it was Caribbean or from Central or South America. Or maybe it was from nowhere. Maybe he'd made it up. Like his name. Delmundo Real. I knew enough high school Spanish to know the first name meant "of the world." I wasn't sure about the "Real."

"What would you like me to tell you?"

"Who you are." He was blunt, and he gazed at me as if he could see through any lie I'd tried to tell.

"You know who I am, Mr. Real. Don't you remember? I'm Tommie Hayes. My friend, the man who manages the hotel, recommended me." I didn't flinch. I didn't blink. I was as cool as I'd ever been in my life. But I could feel my bottom lip begin to tremble. He smiled as if he knew something I didn't and leaned back against his chair, studying my face, taking me in slowly, as if he had all the time in the world. I heard a sudden, loud burst of laughter from one of the rooms, and I jumped involuntarily, then willed my heart to be still. There was more laughter; a man spoke roughly, in what sounded like a foreign language. The words and the tone of his voice were gruff and ugly with no humor in them. I heard a scream but couldn't tell if it was one of terror or pleasure. I would call the cops when I got back to my room, I decided. But what would I tell them?

"What do you think I do here?" he asked. His voice was polite, charming.

I tried to shrug lightly, but my shoulders moved awkwardly and felt as if they didn't belong to me. "Play cards. Party hearty. Stuff most people like to do." I managed to bop my head, nodding as I spoke, like a woman with nothing on her mind but playing cards and partying hearty.

"What else?" His eyes bored into me.

"I have no idea, Mr. Real, and whatever it is is certainly none of my business." I widened mine, trying hard for innocence.

"I get things for people," he said, as if he owed me an explanation. "I get things that are hard to find and that nobody else can get. Special things for people with certain acquired tastes." He snickered when he said that, as if it were his own private joke. My blood ran cold. I tried to force a smile. My lips were numb.

"Like a personal shopper in a department store?" I finally said, like some kind of a fool, which was how I wanted to sound. Just another dumb broad, too dumb to know or remember anything important. Too dumb to care one way or the other.

"So what brings you to Atlantic City, a pretty woman like you. Smart woman like you. You have nothing better to do with your time and mind than tend bars?"

"I like tending bars and making fast cash. I like the city, too." God knew why I'd added that. He was on it like white on rice.

"Why do you like this filthy city?"

"I used to come here when I was a kid," I said, for some reason repeating Jayne Lucindo's words to me about herself and Layne Grimaldi.

"Where did you go here when you were a kid?"

"Lot of places." I tried desperately to remember the names of places I'd heard of. "It was a long time ago, though. I used to come here to the beach. We used to call it Chicken Bone Beach then. My daddy used to be a bouncer, worked a couple of clubs on the North Side. But I grew up down South with my mother. Came here during the summer. That was why I came." Was he satisfied? I wondered. It was impossible to read what lay in those eyes.

"How long will you stay?"

"Long enough to make some money."

"So what do you want from me, Delmundo Real, this department store personal shopper?" He smiled a pretty smile that made his face look more innocent than he had ever been in his life. I thought about what Louella Wallace had called him. "Answer me!" His eyes were angry now, contemptuous, and I knew then that he was playing a game I couldn't win.

But how much did he know and who had told him?

Why not just come out straight and ask me what I was doing down here, what I was looking for? Did he think I was investigating him?

"Well, you could start by telling me if you want me to work for you tonight, Mr. Real. I'd appreciate knowing because I might have to cancel some plans. Make some other arrangements." I played his game. I didn't have a choice. A frightened mouse knocked around by a stalking cat.

"You'll know soon enough." He stood up abruptly and walked out on his terrace as if he needed some air.

"So you were out here?" He turned to see my reaction. My heart stopped.

"Yes. For a moment. It's a beautiful day." My voice was shaking. I prayed he couldn't tell.

I tried to think of some reason not to join him out there if he asked, and then felt silly for being afraid. He wasn't stupid enough to throw me off a terrace in broad daylight. He stepped back and closed the door.

"You can go now," he said.

"Well, it's been nice talking to you," I said dumbly, knowing I sounded foolish and not giving a damn one way or the other, just wanting to get out of there as quickly as I could.

But he wasn't finished with me yet. "Oh, by the way, did you get my flowers?"

I stood stunned as I tried to make sense of what he'd just said.

"Did you get my flowers?" He repeated the question, demanding an answer. It was the same question Basil had asked me a week ago, and that thought was dizzying.

"No." From somewhere, I found my voice.

"The roses that were brought to you this morning?"

"Yes," I heard myself say, but the voice didn't belong to me. Without acknowledging my answer or giving me another glance or word, he left the room, his bare feet making no sound on the thick rug. Somehow I got out of there. I'm not to this day sure how. But one thought crowded out all others.

He knows my name.

I rode the elevator down, my heart pounding, my breath tight at the top of my throat. The bellman had asked if I was Tamara Hayle, not Tommie Hayes.

What else did he know about me?

Both Amaretta and Jayne Lucindo knew about my son. Why had I told them? How could I have been so careless?

I don't remember changing elevators or pressing the button or even opening the door to my room. I slammed the door behind me, scarcely breathing until I put on the double lock. I ripped the flowers from the box where I'd left them on the bureau, threw them on the floor, and they lay scattered, a red mess of blossoms and stems as I searched in vain for a card that didn't exist. A handful at a time, I jammed them into my narrow trash can, wiping my hands as I did so, as if something dirty from his hands lingered on each stem.

And then it caught my eye. One stem stripped clean of leaves lay tucked under tissue in the bottom of the box. The flower that had crowned it was broken off and placed beside it. Its delicate petals had been ripped away from its fragile yellow base, and it lay naked and vulnerable, like some fragile creature whose wings have been shorn.

7

I was the mouse to Delmundo Real's cat, and I could still feel the sting of his claws on my tender behind. After I threw away the roses, I closed the drapes, snatching them shut with so much force I snapped the plastic pull. Then I called my son. Annie picked up the phone. She could hear the panic rising in my voice so she handed the phone to Jamal without a scolding word about me being overprotective. When I heard him speak, I just listened to his voice, cherishing the sound of it as he rattled on about ordinary things. When he finished giving me the details of a history test he'd aced and a basketball game he'd lost, I told him why I called. I explained that I was dealing with some nasty characters and that I wanted him to be

careful, to spend all of his free time over at Annie's, to stay away from our house until I got back.

"Nasty characters? Ma, what do you mean?"

"Well." I paused, not sure how to explain. "You
know what I mean, son. Just be very careful. Don't
take any chances."

"No, Ma. I don't know what you mean. Spell it
out."

"Stay at Annie's. Don't hang out at night. Don't
talk to strangers."

"Have you forgotten? I'm a young black man,
strangers don't talk to *me*," he said, and I smiled
despite myself. Recently, we'd begun to discuss
the negative, fearful ways in which so many people regard young black men. We laughed about it,
but our levity always had a bitter edge.

"Well, do the other two."

He was silent and then said, "So what are you
doing down there anyway?"

"Working a case, you know that."

"It's a dumb way to make a living, Ma. And I'm
not trying to be fresh or anything but I don't see
why you can't have a normal job like everybody
else." His voice had the usual degree of grumpi-
ness it has these day whenever we talk about the
way I earn my living. My profession has become a
tense topic of discussion between us recently. He
didn't think about it much when he was young,

but now it worries him. I could almost see him pursing his lips. "It's dangerous. We're always broke. Do you know anybody else who drives a car as broke-down and embarrassing as the Blue Demon? Half the time, the people you work for don't appreciate what you've done for them. Why, Ma? Why?"

"Jamal, let's not start—" I stuttered out, but there was no stopping him.

"Why can't you be a secretary or a clerk or a chef or something like that? It's not too late. You can still go back to school. Or maybe you could work in a beauty shop like Ms. Green. I'll bet she could use some help around the Biscuit doing people's hair. Or maybe you could be a consultant like Aunt Annie. She makes a lot of money. Anything would be better than what you do. I worry about you, Ma. Out there all by yourself. I worry about you!"

I held the phone without saying anything, struck by the distress in my son's voice. "Jamal, you know how tough I am, and that I can take care of myself," I said, trying to reassure him. My response had the ring of truth because it was, and Jamal knew it. He'd seen me in action on at least one occasion. "Can you really see me waiting on a table or answering somebody's phone? You know how easily silly folks get on my nerves. I'd be fired before the day was out. And as for hair, half the time, I don't take good care of my own. Wyvetta would be a fool to put me in charge of somebody else's, and we both know that Wyvetta Green is nobody's fool. And cooking? You've seen me in a kitchen. You're a better cook than I am, right?"

"That's true," he admitted.

"Don't worry about me, son. Promise me you won't."

"Yeah, like you don't worry about me." I could hear humor creeping into his voice. I smiled at the sound of it.

"If I promise to worry less about you, then you'll try not to worry about me, okay?"

"Then can I go over to the house and work on my computer?"

"Definitely not." I wasn't making any deals.

"Didn't you just say you won't worry about me if I don't worry about you?"

The older he got the harder his head got. "You can work on Annie's computer."

"That old-ass thing—"

"Watch your mouth."

"Sorry. But what am I supposed to do over at Annie's? She doesn't even have cable!" We'd entered the whiny stage.

"Try reading," I said, then cautiously got back to the real issue, the one I knew was bothering him. "I'm a private investigator, son. This is what I do for a living. Sometimes, I wish I could do something else but this is where I am now, this is how I support us. It's what I do best, and I have to ask you to accept that. Okay?"

"Nothing I could say would make a difference anyway."

"Everything you say makes a difference, you know that."

There was another pause. "Ma?"

"Yeah."

"I love you."

"I love you, too, son. Take care of yourself." After he hung up, I sat there awhile longer thinking about what he had said and wishing he was grown enough to tell him everything that was on my mind. The truth was that at the end of the day, all of it, every bit of it was for him. Who else did I have? If there was danger, then I'd have to deal with it. This was what I did and would always do. Sometimes I wish it was different, but this is my reality. And the truth of it was, I enjoyed it. I loved what I did. There was nothing else I was suited to do.

But arguing with Jamal had been like arguing with myself, and I couldn't pretend that I wasn't uneasy. There was always danger in my work, and Delmundo Real was simply the latest flavor. It scared the hell out of me to think that he knew who I was. He was the kind of man who would go for my jugular if he thought I was a threat, and I was sure that was what he thought. Why else would I have been working undercover? Should I leave the hotel? I wondered. Maybe it was time for me simply to check out, stay somewhere else. But instinct told me it would do no good to run. Atlantic City just wasn't that big. Besides that, the Desmonds had already paid my expenses here. What would it look like if I turned tail and ran at the first sign of trouble?

Would my search for Gabriella Desmond inevitably lead me to a confrontation with Delmundo Real?

Should I have told the man the truth? I wondered. Maybe I should have pretended that I thought he was a legitimate businessman. I could have smiled in his face, apologized for lying to him in the first place, and asked him if he'd ever heard of a teenager named Gabriella Desmond. He would have told me no. I could have said, Thank you very much, sir, sorry to have bothered you, and continued with my fruitless search in conventional places. At the end of the week, I could have explained to the Desmonds that I couldn't find their daughter, billed them for my fee, suggested that they call the cops, and that would have been the end of it. Delmundo Real's business could have stayed his own. I wouldn't be afraid then. I wouldn't have had to call my son and beg him to be careful.

Except that from her very first words, Amaretta had touched me. She was somebody's lost child and deserved to be looked out for. Somehow or other Amaretta was tied to Delmundo Real as surely as she was tied to Gabriella Desmond, and sooner or later I would probably have to face him down if I was going to help her. Hopefully, it would be later. Much later.

I felt tense for the rest of the day, spent a fitful Saturday night and made my way to church on Sunday morning; it never hurts to pray. Bright and early Monday, I headed to the public library to do some research. The librarian at the front desk was a plump, honey-colored woman whose eyes lit up when she casually asked me my profession and I told her I was a vacationing private investigator.

"We don't get many of those in here," she said, admiration shining in her eyes behind her tortoiseshell glasses. "I certainly envy you such an exciting profession!"

"It has its moments," I said, wishing Jamal was around to hear this new perspective. She pointed me toward a research area complete with computers, printers and various reference books. I sat down and began to go through files of the local and state newspapers looking for information on Gabriel Wallace and Delmundo Real. There were photos of Wallace leading demonstrations but little else of importance. I turned up nothing on Delmundo Real, which didn't really surprise me. I went back a year looking for anything I could find about suicides—specifically young girls jumping off buildings—and finally found something.

An article in one of the local papers reported that an unidentified woman, who may have been a teenage runaway, had committed suicide by jumping off the balcony of an unidentified hotel. The story ran about a column and a half on the back page and that was that. It ran next to a story about the increase in homeless teenagers in Atlantic City, which I read with interest.

The story on runaways referred to the kids as "throwaways," children with no family or home to speak of, who were forced to live in the underbelly of the city. It described how they huddled under the boardwalk for food and washed in the empty rest rooms of casinos, forming their own little families to protect and care for one another. They were elusive, it reported, the hardest to reach among the homeless. They often didn't trust adults because their parents had betrayed them, and they ran away because they could not live safely at home. Many of them had been physically abused or sexually molested. Their lives at home were often living hells, and they had nowhere to go but the streets. Atlantic City represented the good life to many of them. It meant fast money and faster times in glamorous casinos. It represented a chance for them to make it on their own. The description didn't seem to fit Gabriella, and I wondered how close it came to describing Rook or Amaretta. I would never know unless I found them.

The librarian, whose name tag read Laura Fuller and who was obviously still curious about me, walked over to check on me after a while. She must have seen the frustration on my face.

"Can I help you with anything specific? Maybe there is another source of information that can be helpful."

"Well, actually, I was looking for information about suicides or murders that have occurred within the last couple of years," I said, hoping for more information on the unidentified girl who had jumped off the roof. My back hurt, and I could feel the muscles in my neck and shoulders tightening. I rubbed them, but it didn't do much good.

"Murder!" Her eyes grew big. "Are you involved in the investigation of the murders of those girls! Well, you know if they weren't poor and black and making a living the best way they could make it, they would have found that man by now." She lifted her head in indignation and continued. "Girls like that are easy prey, but once he gets tired of hunting them, he'll come looking for the rest of us." She leaned forward confidentially, lowering her voice. "You know it's about time for another killing."

"Really?" I forgot about the suicide of the girl and listened with interest. I wondered if she'd overheard somebody talking or seen something in one of the papers I'd missed.

"He strikes around this time every month. You can start to feel the tension in the air when it's time for another one." She glanced around the nearly empty library with worried, suspicious eyes. "I'm sure a man like that doesn't come around here, but you never know."

"What are folks in town saying?" I asked, letting her know by the inflection in my voice that I wondered what black people in town were saying. Like the folks in my hometown, I knew they would have their own particular slant.

"Well." She raised her eyebrows slightly, and her voice took on the cadence that black women often have when we talk among ourselves. "Folks are saying they think the cops know who it is but just don't want to say, and because it's *black* working girls nobody gives a damn one way or the other, and that whoever it is is probably too hot to touch."

"So folks say the killer might be somebody wealthy and powerful?"

"You know as well as I do that if he were black or Hispanic and he was killing white girls, they would have picked his butt up after the first killing. It's like what they used to say about Jack the Ripper, that they never got him because they didn't want to when Scotland Yard found out he was a member of the Royal Family. Well, folks say the same thing about this one here, that the cops know who it is but are just letting him run his course, like they did the Ripper."

"But Jack the Ripper's victims were all prostitutes, and his killing spree was in a particular area and there was a definite pattern. This one's different. His last victim was white," I said, repeating what I'd read in the newspapers.

Laura Fuller was unconvinced. "You can't trust these newspapers because they get their facts from the cops and you can't trust these cops for nothing," she said. "Cops will tell you something is white, and you know it's probably black. Cops will tell you it's morning when you know the sun just set. For all we know that girl could have been a lightskinned black woman. We come in all kinds of shades. I have a great-aunt whose hair is so blond she could pass for Swedish. Cops don't know nothing about black folks except how to pick them up."

I was amused by her jaundiced view of the police and how when it came to the cops, she shed her mantle of proper professionalism and became just another sister off the block.

"Maybe you're right," I said, allowing her suspicions although I didn't share them. I often have my doubts about the veracity of the police, but in this case, I believed them. There are far more good cops than crooked ones, and from personal experience I know how frustrating it is as a police officer to have to deal with a case as difficult as this one. But our conversation reminded me of the importance of finding Gabriella Desmond as quickly as I could. The thought of that brought me back to another reason I'd come to the library.

"There actually is another piece of research I'd like to do while I'm here," I said. "About a wealthy family who once lived in this area."

"Black or white?"

"Black. The Desmonds."

"As in Carver Desmond? We have an entire shelf on him. Let me show it to you. But if you want to know the real history, stop by on your way out and I'll tell you what you *really* need to know," she added with a smile sly enough for me to consider skipping the books altogether.

I followed her to a corner of the library that featured books of local interest. The word "shelf" had been an exaggeration but there were enough books and pamphlets to keep me busy for a while. After she left, I began to go through them, looking over the titles: *The Making of a Negro Millionaire—The Life and Times of Carver Desmond; How I Did It: The Autobiography of Carver Desmond; Money the Old-Fashioned Way—How Carver Desmond Made His Mark*. I picked up one and then another and quickly leafed through them. Most of the books dealt with Carver Desmond's business acumen and his strategies for making a buck. But the self-published *How I Did It* seemed to offer more so I went through it slowly. The language was flowery and pretentious, and I was amazed by the man's seemingly endless capacity for self-aggrandizement. I quickly turned to the shortest chapter, one entitled simply "Personal Life," which gave well-known facts about his dead parents and extended family and closed with the following paragraph:

I HAVE NEVER PERMITTED MYSELF TO INDULGE IN THE URGENT NEEDS THAT SO OFTEN BESET MEN OF HIGH CHARACTER. THESE BASE URGES, WHICH INVARIABLY DEFINE OR DESTROY THE STRONGEST AMONG US, ARE BEST DEALT WITH SWIFTLY, SECRETLY AND AS EFFICIENTLY AS POSSIBLE.

Carver Desmond didn't clarify what he meant by "base urges" and exactly what he did to satisfy them, but it didn't take a genius to figure it out. The man hadn't married, so he was probably a regular patron of the local bordello, wherever that was. It seemed like every hero these days had clay feet if you poked hard enough. But there were certainly worse ways to satisfy those "base urges."

The last book, *Money the Old-Fashioned Way*, was the most recently published, and there was a short section near the end of the text on his last years. Remembering what Gabriel Wallace had told me about his death and that of Foster Desmond's first wife, I looked for some reference to the closeness of their deaths, but there was no mention of either. There was, however, a photograph of the family. It had been taken when Carver Desmond, the young nephew, was a boy. He sat on the floor, squeezed against his mother's knee like a favorite pet who enjoyed being stroked. Dorothea's raven hair fell to her shoulders in an old-fashioned, Veronica Lake hairstyle, and even in this photograph I could clearly see how pretty she was. Her eyes were big and opened wide, and her tiny hand pulled her young son close. Surprisingly, her husband, Foster Desmond, wasn't in this "family" picture, and I wondered where he was. The three of them were dressed in white, as if they'd just stepped in from a game of tennis or golf. None of them was smiling. There was an old-fashioned look to the photo, as if it belonged to another age. The boy looked about eleven, so it must have been taken roughly five years before his mother and uncle died. I went back to the computer for more information about the family but found nothing new.

On the way out of the library, I stopped by the front desk to thank Laura Fuller for her help.

"So did you find what you needed?"

"Well—" I paused, involuntarily revealing my sense of frustration.

"What you need to know about the Desmonds you won't find in these books," she said with the look of a woman who has something to say.

I decided to take her up on it. "Do you have time for lunch?" I glanced at the clock. I'd been here longer than I thought; it was half past noon. "You were so helpful, and I have a while before my next appointment. I'd love to buy you a sandwich or at least a cup of coffee."

She looked doubtful for a moment, then said, as if trying to convince herself, "Might be nice. Nobody has bought me lunch in a long time. I've never really had a chance to talk to a private investigator. Might be fun." She gave me a wide grin. "There's a little diner right across the street if

that's okay with you. Let me tell my supervisor."
She rose and went down the hall to another office,
peeked into it, exchanged a few words and then
came back out. I thanked her for joining me and
meant it. I needed to be reminded of the "glam-
our" of my job as much as I needed to find out the
"real deal" on the Desmonds. But as we walked
across the street, I wondered if it was ethical to
spend the Desmonds' money on idle gossip about
them. On the other hand, it might help me find
their lost daughter. Every little bit helps.

We chatted for a while about my life, how I
ended up in the profession and the ups and
downs I suffered. I embellished a tale or two but
mostly stuck to the truth. I suspected that she was
an avid reader of crime fiction, which was why
she was so curious about me, and she confessed as
much by the time our lunch—tuna fish sand-
wiches and cups of the soup du jour—was placed
in front of us. Leaning forward and speaking confidentially, she asked who I was working for, and I
told her that I wasn't at liberty to say. I explained
my interest in the Desmonds by claiming to be a
history buff who enjoyed researching local histor-
ical figures when I visited various parts of the
state, and that Carver Desmond and his family
had interested me for some time. Fortunately, the
books I'd just skimmed about his life and times

gave me enough superficial information to sound like I knew what I was talking about. She seemed to buy it.

"Well, then you know about the coffins?" she said, between bites of her sandwich.

"You mean the ones that made Desmond a millionaire?" I took a sip of the soup du jour, which I discovered, to my horror, was cream of tomato, my least favorite soup. Only half-listening to her, I considered sending it back.

"You know those things weren't nothing but cheap plywood painted up to look like oak or mahogany. Nothing but junk the white folks wouldn't take. He got it cheap from his rich white friends and pushed it on us and that was what we buried our loved ones in. Most folks didn't know any better." She shook her head in disgust and took a slow, almost meditative sip of soup. "It's terrible the way we can treat our own."

"I had no idea," I said, putting my spoon in my cup and pushing it to the side. I thought about my grandmother and how she kept the fan from his funeral parlors taped to her mirror until the day she died. This revelation was worse than knowing he visited whorehouses. "Are you sure?"

"Yeah, I'm sure. He was nothing but a greedy, mean old bastard," she said like a woman who knows exactly what she is talking about. "My mother had tales about that man that would burn your ears. That's why I smiled when you said you were looking for information about him. People around here will laugh in your face if you say his name with too much reverence. There are still folks walking and breathing to this day who he cheated or deceived, folks who really *knew* the Desmonds."

"And what exactly did they know?" I leaned toward her, my interest piqued.

"How terrible they were," she said quietly. "They just took and took and took from our people and never gave anything back. They bled the folks around here as dry as beans, did us worse than the white folks did us, and because the Desmonds were our own it hurt us more."

"But they were businessmen," I suggested cautiously. "Businessmen are about money, not racial solidarity."

"Humph!" she said with a snort. "Well, there's racial solidarity and there's *racial solidarity*. Smart businessmen know the difference."

"What do you mean by that?"

"I mean most black businesses around here made money, but they didn't forget who helped them make it. They didn't forget where they came from. The Desmonds were another matter."

A watched pot never boils, so I let this one simmer, waiting until it bubbled. "They wouldn't hire dark-skinned people to work anywhere but in their kitchen. You've heard of the old paper bag test, haven't you?" she said with a raised eyebrow and a sneer as she sipped her soup.

I told her that I had. As late as the 1950s there were black folks so color-struck they wouldn't associate with other black people if their skin was darker than a brown paper bag.

"Just think of where we'd be as a people if all of those with money and power and not just a precious few had used their privilege to build institutions that would help us all instead of wasting so much time and money trying to out-white the white man." She shook her head in disgust. "The Desmonds built cheap caskets for their own people and used the money from those and their lousy hotels to pretend they were something they weren't. They never gave a red cent to charity, and God knows we needed it. Churches, Ladies' Aid Societies, nobody could count on doodley-squat from them. They'd give money to poor white folks before they'd give it to poor black ones. The Desmonds liked to think they were high-born, but they were low-down as lice, all that meanness and stinginess will come back on you, won't it?" she added with a self-satisfied cackle. I wondered if the disappearance of Gabriella had become common knowledge, and I asked her what she meant.

"The old man dying of a stroke like he did, and

the wife, Dorothea, dying the very next day. That old man was a nasty ole something or other. My mother used to say the whole family had problems, though, and the things that went on in that household were enough to straighten my nappy hair. She never could bring herself to tell me what they were," she added, anticipating my next question. "Mama always did have a flair for the dramatic, if you know what I mean," she added with a bitter-sweet smile that told me her memories of her mother were loving ones.

"What kind of woman was Dorothea?"

"She was a silly little rich girl, the kind that Ida Desmond would have approved of and chosen. She was pampered, and never had to do anything for herself. Spoiled and selfish. Mama knew people who worked there, and they used to say that the woman was crazy. She looked like a white woman, the way pretty black women were supposed to look in those days. Very weak, very dependent. That's probably why Foster was never around. She was like a child, couldn't do nothing without him."

"What do you mean?"

"He made it his business to stay out of that house. For months sometimes, he wouldn't be there. Mama said Dorothea would just wring her hands and cry because she was so unhappy. The only thing that brought her joy was her boy,

Carver. She used to call him 'Manny,' used to say he was her little man, fed him treats like he was her little toy dog."

"How do people feel about the family now?" I wondered if her take on the Desmonds was the common one. Laura shrugged as she finished up her soup and wiped her mouth daintily with the edge of a napkin.

"I don't think anybody thinks too much about them one way or the other these days. The old man and his evil ways, whatever they were, is dead and gone. His sister is dead. His younger brother is still alive, but most folks just felt sorry for him when his wife died, doing herself in like she did. I think he must have felt guilty about her death, staying away so much, neglecting her and the boy. Some say he drove her to it."

"Do you mean that Dorothea Desmond killed herself?"

"Slashed her wrist in one of their big fancy bathrooms the day after the uncle died. Her 'little man' found her."

I'm not sure what emotion showed on my face, but I knew what was in my heart. I had found my brother Johnny all those years ago, the morning after he'd taken his own life, and the horror of that day still played itself out in my dreams. I couldn't catch my breath for a moment. I made myself listen to Laura, forcing down the past as I often have to do. Trying to make that image of my brother that has taken root in my brain disappear.

"But you know how black folks are. We're not a people to hold a grudge or we'd begrudge the world," she continued philosophically. "But I guess that's neither here nor there, is it? The younger brother did change some after those two deaths. He married a local girl, and I hear he stays at home now. Trying to make up for the other one, I guess. I heard he's tried to be a father to his step-daughter, trying to make up for that, too. I guess the boy got over all that trauma and is doing all right. You don't hear much about him, one way or the other. Must be in his twenties by now."

I nodded that she was right.

"Things just keep going on. Like people do," she added. "Forgetting the past, moving toward the future."

"Except the future is always found in the past," I said, thinking about Dorothea's son and feeling the deep swift pain I feel whenever the past of my brother's death hits me in my present. I understood young Carver Desmond's spirit now with all of its awkwardness and desperate need to find his lost sister. We talked awhile longer, about this that and nothing, but my mind stayed on Carver Desmond and the legacy that must haunt him as surely as mine did me.

8

I didn't recognize Louella Wallace when I saw her. She didn't look like the shy woman who told me her secrets the week before and whose spiteful, parting words had shocked me. She was dressed in a drab blue suit more fitting for an office than a bar and sat near a group of slot machines. She had two shot glasses filled with liquor before her, and a cigarette burning in an ashtray. She looked stiff and uncomfortable in her high-backed chair as she nervously surveyed the room.

It was late Friday afternoon, four days after I talked to Laura Fuller in the library. Nothing had changed. I was still headed nowhere down the same nowhere road. I'd driven by Jayne Lucindo's house Wednesday night with no luck. The only thing my countless strolls down the boardwalk hoping to run into Gabriella or her boyfriend had earned me were sore feet. I was disgusted, discouraged and depressed, and there's nothing much you can do when you feel that way except eat. Hunger had forced me into the hotel lobby in search of an early dinner.

Most of the patrons at the bar looked like office workers in TGIF mode stopping by for a quick shot of bourbon and a chance to grab some luck. Louella Wallace fit right in. I watched her for a few moments, wondering what she was up to and how long she'd been sitting there. After about fifteen minutes something caught her eye, and I followed her gaze across the room.

The object of her attention was a slightly built, wiry kid who stood about five foot six. His skin was a rich cocoa brown and his eyes were round like a doll's. His hair was braided in tight cornrows on either side of his narrow face, which had delicate features as pretty as a girl's. But what he lacked in macho looks, he made up for in don't-fuck-with-me swagger. His baggy pants swung low off his behind and his black belt with its heavy gold buckle looked as if it could barely keep them up. His oversized FUBU football jersey was dark blue with a large white "05" on the front, and a big gold filigreed chain sparkled around his neck. His white sneakers were so clean they shone. He walked with a slight limp, what Dominique Desmond might have called a wolf's lope, but that reminded me of that slow, easy stroll folks in my brother's generation called a "pimp." I wondered where he had learned it, and if he was as tough as he tried to look. I was sure he was Cardell Cummings, the notorious Rook.

He didn't smile, not even when he sat down at Louella Wallace's table. There was no hint of recognition or acknowledgment when she handed him a manila envelope. He just slipped it into a pocket in his baggy jeans and buttoned it closed. Still without speaking, he slipped on a pair of narrow sunglasses and left, pausing at one of the slot machines long enough to slip in a quarter. Louella lit a cigarette and finished up her drink. I waited a few minutes and followed him outside.

He walked leisurely down the boardwalk as if he had nowhere else to go. Every now and then he stopped to bum a cigarette from another kid or converse with other teenagers leaning against the railing, staying only long enough to give somebody a high-five or a hug. I was struck by the easy camaraderie between these kids. They formed the families they didn't have, as the article I'd read in the library had said, protecting one another, nurturing as best they could. What choice did they have? A kid was legally an adult at eighteen, even if he had nowhere to go, no resources or safety net to soften a fall.

Nothing but a nigger.

I got angry again just thinking about Carver Desmond's words. He would never have to know life as this boy knew it. He was privileged and protected by his family's name and money, although that brought its own cruel legacy, too, I reminded myself. But it still seemed unfair.

Rook stopped at a stand lined with stuffed animals and toy rifles and watched several tourists take turns shooting for a stuffed bear. I bought a raspberry Italian ice from a wagon, took a few licks and then leisurely strolled in his direction. By the time I reached him, he was holding the gun himself, preparing to try his luck. I stood in the group of about five people and watched him shoot. He missed the first couple of times and then bagged it on his third try. The crowd applauded, and he tucked his prize, a red-and-white teddy bear, under his arm and continued on his way. In his excitement, he left his sunglasses on the counter. I picked them up and slipped them into my Kenya bag. He walked about another five minutes and then stopped by a food stand, took out a handful of change, counted it carefully and bought a hot dog, settling down on a nearby bench to eat it, cramming it into his mouth, wiping away the dripping mustard with the back of his hand.

I was sure that the envelope he'd gotten from Louella was filled with money. What else could it be? I was also sure it was for Gabriella. But he'd stopped on the way to win her a bear, counted his change carefully to buy himself some dinner, and left her money untouched. Jayne was right; he took care of her. I wondered if he was on his way home. I considered following him, but then changed my mind. He could wander around for the rest of the afternoon, and I wanted to get back to the casino to catch Louella. The drinks lined up in front of her hinted that she'd be there awhile.

"Excuse me." I pulled out the sunglasses as I approached him. "I think these belong to you. You dropped them a few minutes ago." Startled, his mouth bulging with food, he glanced up, searched his pocket for the missing glasses and then grabbed them from me.

"Thanks." He slipped them on. He had a sweet face, but I'd known kids with sweeter faces who could cut your throat without a second thought. I took a few licks off my ice.

"Anybody sitting here?"

He looked surprised but didn't object. "Knock yourself out." His voice was deep, already that of a man. I put his age at eighteen, but not much more than that. I picked up and held the toy bear that lay between us.

"Cute."

"Thanks."

"Whoever you won it for is really going to like it." He studied me for a few moments as if he were deciding whether he should talk to me or not.

"How you know I didn't win it for myself?"

"Because it's the kind of toy you win for a kid, or somebody who's about to have a kid," I said, dead serious. He stared at me without saying anything. I licked the last of my raspberry ice and threw it away, and he watched it drop into the wastebasket, his eyes following it as it toppled in. "They call you Rook, right?"

He looked scared. "What you want?"

"To talk to you."

He stood up. "You a cop?"

"No." I put my hand on his arm, trying to reassure him. He jerked away, but didn't run away and I considered it a victory. "My name is Tamara Hayle. I'm a private investigator. I'm looking for Gabriella Desmond. I've talked to Amaretta and Jayne Lucindo. I'd like to talk to you if you'll let me."

Neither of us moved for a few moments. A girl about eleven ran by chasing a beach ball. A gull, squawking loudly, dove for a discarded french fry. I watched it take off and fly into the distance.

"I know you know where she is, and I'm going to find her sooner or later," I said. "But it's better if

I find her now. She could be in a lot of trouble, and I want to help her."

"What kind of trouble?" A shadow seemed to pass over his face.

"I just need to talk to her."

"Who sent you?" He searched my face. "The Desmonds?" Real fear replaced the shadow, and he pulled away.

"No," I said quickly.

"Who then?"

"I used to work at the mission down the street. She stopped in there once, and somebody said I could find her through you." I was playing it by ear and hoped I had it right.

He was good at hiding what was on his mind. I could tell he didn't trust people easy; he didn't trust me. I wondered what had brought him to the street, but I knew if I asked he wouldn't tell me. I was lucky I'd gotten this much out of him, and that he hadn't followed his first impulse and bolted. I remembered what Jayne had said about him.

Where does he live?

Hell if I know.

"Like I said, I talked to Jayne Lucindo," I added. "She said you took good care of Gabriella. I can see that you do."

He relaxed a little, took a breath. "How long you known Jayne?"

"A while."

"You know where she is?" There was concern in his eyes now, replacing the worry.

"I haven't seen her for a few days." He took out a cigarette and smoked it, holding it between his thumb and forefinger like tough guys do in gangster movies, taking deep, fast drags and blowing the smoke out through his nose.

"I gotta go." He gave me a quick sideways glance.

"To give Gabriella her money?"

"How'd you know I had some money?" He snuffed out his cigarette, turning his gaze on me, his eyes narrow and mean with suspicion.

"I saw you get it from Louella."

"You lying then. You know about that, you lying! They sent you, didn't they? How long you been following me?" He snatched the toy I'd been holding from my hand and tucked it back under his arm, backing away from me.

I softened my voice when I spoke. "I know what the two of you are going through. Being a father for the first time is a very scary thing, Cardell. It's something—"

When he turned to face me, his eyes were wild with rage and his voice so choked he couldn't get his words out. "Who told you I gave Gabriella that baby? I ain't never touched Gabriella that way. I would never touch Gabriella like that. Never!" His small body shook with rage, and then he turned and ran, his white sneakers pounding the pavement so loud and fast there was no way I could have caught him even if I wanted to.

I went back to the casino as empty-handed as I'd left it. But I'd met the kid whom she'd run off with, and he'd told me that her baby wasn't his and I believed him. Louella Wallace was still sitting at her table as I thought she would be, and I went over to where she was sitting.

"Mind if I join you?" She glanced at me meekly, then dropped her eyes, embarrassed. I sat down, ordered a glass of wine and got to the point quickly. "How come you gave Gabriella's boyfriend that money? Why didn't you tell me you knew him before?"

She took a sip of her drink. "Gabriella called me and said she was going to send him over to pick up some money from me. That's all. I'm trying to help the girl out."

"It's from her father?"

She stared ahead, her mouth set in a hard, straight line.

"Does her mother know?"

"You didn't find Gabriella yet, did you?" There was a taunting edge in her voice that told me she knew that I hadn't and wasn't about to.

"You know where she is, don't you?"

"Life has taught me to never tell everything I know." She touched my hand as if consoling me. Her touch made me uneasy. A sly smile spread on her face. She left without another word or glance. I watched her go, thinking what a strange, secretive woman she was and stunned by what a vicious streak she had.

I finished off my wine in one gulp, still shaken by that encounter, and then ordered a turkey club and treated myself to a slice of apple pie, realizing how hungry I was. I ate fast, wolfing the food down the way Rook had devoured that hot dog, like it would be the last meal I'd get in this or any other life. Then I ordered another glass of wine and sipped it slowly, feeling sorry for myself and wondering if I was going to get any kind of a break at all. The longer I was in this city, the more questions I had and the harder answers were to find.

As I waited for the elevator to go back to my room, my thoughts returned to still another piece of this puzzle, the one with an edge sharp enough to kill, the one that didn't fit with any of the other pieces: Delmundo Real. I knew I would hear from him again, and I didn't like to think about it. One more question with no answer to it. When the elevator came, I stepped in, hardly aware of the two women who stood against the wall.

"I just know one thing, honey. I'm going up to my room, pack and get out of this town as soon as I can cash in my chips," said the tall one. Caught up in my thoughts, I only half-listened. But I did wonder what madness would make a grown woman dress in orange and yellow polka dots.

"I don't blame you, girl, I just don't want to be next," said her friend, who wore a pale, seafoam-green suit. She was short and plump and had a round pleasant face that reminded me of Annie's.

"Why would the man pick you, Delores?"

"Well, you never know, Pam. You never can tell about crazy people. I'm so sick and tired of these damn nuts! They're always doing something they ain't got no business doing. I'm just sick and tired of them!"

"A person can't help being crazy, Delores. I just wished they'd leave the rest of us alone. There's enough of them in this world for them to pick on each other instead of the rest of us."

They nodded their heads, united in disgust.

"Did you hear about what happened?" Pam in polka dots turned to include me in the conversation in the familiar way black women do when we find ourselves alone in a public place.

"No. What?"

"Well, he got somebody else!"

"Number six," the woman in green chimed in. "And you know that's an unlucky number."

Polka dots turned back to her friend. "I don't know about six being so unlucky, Delores. Seven is supposed to be lucky, but I've never heard anything about six being unlucky. Seven. Eleven. Those are lucky numbers."

"Well, six was unlucky for that poor girl."

My blood ran cold.

"Came on the TV, right before I left my room." Polka dots turned to me again. "The sixth one. Puerto Rican. Killed her right in her own room, within walking distance of this hotel." She turned back to her friend. "He could have been hanging around here for all we know. Standing next to us. Playing the slots! Waiting to kill some innocent somebody! See what I mean about these god-damned crazy people!"

"Time for us to go. Get the hell out of Dodge!" the woman in green said, and both women chuckled as they got off at their floor. I stood still, not even aware that the elevator doors had closed.

Jayne Lucindo.

I bolted the door when I got to my room, turned on the TV, switched channels until I found the report.

Jayne Lucindo, twenty, had become the murderer's sixth and latest victim. She had been found dead in her two-bedroom apartment just blocks from the boardwalk and the casinos. She had been beaten and then shot in the face. But according to the coroner, the gunshot had not caused her death; the beating had. The police also revealed for the first time that the shot to the head had followed the beating in at least one other case. For all intents and purposes, the killer had shot at point-blank range somebody whom he had already killed, the coroner observed. I closed my eyes and tried to imagine her face as I had seen it ten days ago—alive and full of sass when she'd told off J.J. But she had been vulnerable and frightened, too. And now she was dead.

Shaken and stammering, J.J. was interviewed on camera. I prayed he wouldn't get carried away by the moment and mention a private detective named Tamara Hayle or a pregnant roommate named Gabriella Desmond. But he was surprisingly reticent, saying simply that he was sorry for her family and for her, and then walking away from the camera with his head down. A report by a police expert followed the interview with J.J. The expert assured the public that his officers were following many leads and that although there were similarities in the six murders, he was not ready to state conclusively that this was the work of one killer. His opinion was countered by that of an expert on serial killers who stated the opposite, then grimly added that the killer seemed to be changing his pattern. He reminded viewers that the victim before this one had also been found in her apartment, so there was a possibility that the killer was getting bolder and taking more chances. He also added that Jayne Lucindo and Layne Grimaldi were acquainted, as were some of the other victims, and that the time between killings was growing shorter. But there was another piece of information they had left out, the piece that I had, and that was that Gabriella Desmond had roomed with them both. Dominique Desmond's intuition was serving her well.

I tried desperately to recall every detail of my conversation with Jayne, everything that she had said about Layne Grimaldi, Gabriella Desmond or the boy I just had left. I tried to remember the details of her bedroom and the small drab apartment. Was there anything I had missed that would have told me that ten days later she would be killed? I thought again about her bed with the fancy lace sheets and the old rag doll that lay on a pillow.

Where do you work?

For a guy who hangs out in the casinos.

So these dates you went on with Layne, what was that about?

We weren't doing men for money, if that's what you're talking about.

Who did you borrow money from?

People we knew.

Why hadn't I pushed her for more concrete information, addresses, telephone numbers? I'd left out the most basic questions. Had Jayne been the mysterious young woman who had called Dominique Desmond and told her where to find her missing daughter?

My mama's dead. She loved me very much but she's dead now.

What kind of a half-stepping, half-assed private investigator was I?

I switched to another channel in time to hear a newswoman ask how anyone could beat a girl brutally enough to kill her. I snapped the television off, answering her question for myself.

Because the killer was trying to get something from her, something he thought she had but wouldn't give up.

Should I go to the police? Was it my professional responsibility to report what I knew about Jayne Lucindo and her connection to Gabriella Desmond and Layne Grimaldi? I thought about it for a while, wrestling with the pros and cons of it and then finally acknowledged something I hate to admit even to myself. Despite once having been a police officer, I dread talking to the cops unless there's absolutely no alternative. Deep in my heart, I don't trust them. I've been close enough to the inner world that cops inhabit to know how many of them harbor suspicious, negative feelings about black people, and how quick some are to assume the worst. I didn't want to involve the police unless I absolutely had to. I didn't want to involve the Desmonds, either. Rich black folks were as suspect to many cops as poor ones, sometimes more so. I had a professional responsibility to my clients, too, not to bring the cops down on them—for any reason.

What could I tell the cops anyway? That I was a private investigator looking for a lost girl who had once lived with two of the murder victims? It would be helpful, if they didn't know, but they probably did. What could I say about Delmundo Real? That I had worked for him as a bartender, and he had sent me some flowers with the heads chopped off and that I was sure he had something to do with all the murdered women? What would the cops make of that? If Jayne Lucindo's murder had been a random act by a serial killer, which was what the cops thought, then it was unrelated to Gabriella's disappearance and if I got involved with their investigation, where would it lead? Would I put myself—or Gabriella—in danger or make us both look suspicious?

But still, I was afraid, and my fear drained me. I crawled into bed underneath the sheets like a scared kid, closed my eyes and tried to erase Jayne

Lucindo's face from my mind. But the image of that rag doll came back to me and that faded into Jamal's stuffed green snake and then, finally, I fell asleep.

I awoke to the phone ringing. I let it ring and then picked it up, thinking it might be Jamal.

"I won't be needing you tonight," said Delmundo Real. I froze at the sound of his voice. "And you got my flowers?" It was the same question spoken in the same tone.

"Why don't you tell me what you want? Tell me what the hell you want from me!" I demanded, masking my fear with bravado.

"Stay away from mine." The phone went dead.

And who was his? Amaretta? Gabriella Desmond? Rook? Had Layne Grimaldi and Jayne Lucindo been his, too?

Somebody knocked. I willed myself to get up, to walk to the door. I stood next to it, listening, my body tense as I prayed whoever was there would go away. But he knocked again, harder this time.

"Tamara, are you there?" he asked. I opened the door to Basil Dupre.

9

"Tamara, what happened?" asked Basil Dupre.

"Nothing!" I've never been a good liar.

"Delmundo Real?"

"How did you know?"

"Do you want to talk about it?"

"I don't know."

"Come with me."

"Where?"

"Does it matter?" He smiled his charming smile because he knew it didn't.

"I'll meet you downstairs in fifteen minutes," I told him.

"No. I'll wait here, outside your door," he said. I was grateful for that.

I dressed quickly, pulling on whatever I could lay my hands on first, not bothering with makeup, hair or anything else. My only concern was getting out—of this room, this hotel, this city—as fast as I could.

We scarcely spoke as we walked through the lobby to the valet parking stand where he called for his car. But I felt safe, and it felt good for a change to accept protection from somebody else, not to have to be the tough one, to allow somebody else to look out for danger. The attendant brought his car, a late model, charcoal-gray BMW, twice as big and four times more powerful than the Blue Demon. I slid into the passenger's side, noticing with annoyance the tender way the parking attendant opened and closed the car door. Never in its tired woebegone life had the Demon received such loving attention from a parking attendant.

I've never been a woman easily seduced by the trappings of a man's wealth or power. His interior world—the strength of his mind, generosity of his spirit, basic integrity—is what interests me. But as I glided through the streets of Atlantic City cradled in the luxury of Basil Dupre's expensive car—each bump in the road made gentle, each grating sound closed out—I could understand how a woman can learn to put up with things she shouldn't for the sake of creature comfort. He drove the car fast but expertly, his attention riveted to the road ahead of us.

"Where do you want to go?"

"I don't know."

We drove for a while longer in silence, and I closed my eyes and listened to the soothing hum of the well-tuned engine. The leather upholstery, as soft as a glove, felt cool and luxurious as I settled into it, and I realized how exhausted this day had left me. My thoughts were a jumble of impressions about Gabriella Desmond, Rook, Louella Wallace and above all Delmundo Real. I was at once frustrated, perplexed and scared to death, and I didn't know where one feeling stopped and another began. It was a clear night, and the moon shone bright and full through the tinted windshield. I made myself concentrate on the stars that shone brightly in the sky. It reminded me of the last time we were together. I smiled at the memory.

"You've done it again," I said.

"Done what?"

"Rescued me. Have you forgotten the last time?" His quick glance in my direction told me he hadn't.

"Our transportation wasn't so comfortable that night," he said. "But the place we ended up in was more beautiful." We'd driven to a villa high in the Blue Mountains of Jamaica, and spent a night together that the thought of still keeps me warm on a cold Jersey night. I wondered if that night had meant as much to him as it did to me. But wasn't that always the question when you shared a night with a man, especially one like Basil Dupre? Maybe in the end it didn't matter. I knew how I felt, and that was all that counted.

"There was less danger there, that night," Basil added after a moment. "Far less to be afraid of."

"So where are you taking me this time?"

"Wherever you want to go."

"Away from here," I said, and added, "away from this city."

"Philadelphia? New York City? Back home to Newark?"

"No. Not home."

"I know a place," he said after a moment. "We can talk there, have a drink later if you like. Then I can take you back to your hotel, if you want to go," he added without making an issue of it. I knew that was a question that would have to be answered before the night was through.

We took a turn onto a side road and another to a highway that led away from the city and drove for half an hour until he pulled into the driveway of an inn, which looked as if it had once been a mansion. The dark paneling and elaborate stained glass windows in the intimate bar where he led me spoke of elegance and mystery. The ceiling was high and the oak floors were buffed to a mirror finish. Period furniture, delicate and expensive, was scattered here and there. We sat at a small corner table dimly lit by candles. From somewhere soft jazz was being played on a piano. I ordered a glass of Pinot Grigio and Basil drank cognac. A slight, mysterious smile appeared on his face. As always, I was bewitched by his eyes.

"You feel better now."

"I'm not afraid anymore," I said, although Basil brought a different kind of danger. "Thank you for bringing me here."

"I enjoy rescuing you."

"I don't want to make a habit of it."

"It's all right with me if you do."

"I don't think it's wise," I said. We both took an anxious sip of our drinks.

He seemed a different Basil Dupre, changed in some subtle way. He had seemed melancholy when I saw him on the boardwalk, and his sadness was more pronounced now. I wondered if it was because of his missing daughter, or maybe simply the passage of time. I know I had changed since the last time we'd been together. I was older certainly, not much wiser, but different in not immediately perceptible ways.

"You are more at home with yourself, Tamara," he said after a while. He stated it evenly, as if it were something he'd just noticed about me. "You're stronger. I can tell that, too, even though I haven't seen you in a long time." I smiled slightly and nodded in agreement, trying not to pass any judgment about the time that had passed and what it did or didn't mean.

"Have you found out anything new about your daughter?" I asked, and the sadness that came into his eyes told me that I shouldn't have. "If I come across anything—" I added, then stopped, as I remembered the girl with the pretty face who had made me think about him. Had she been his daughter?

"I don't want you to get involved," he interrupted me. "Promise me that you won't. My daughter is my responsibility. I've failed her for a long time, and finding her will help me set things straight with myself and honor the memory of her mother. I have to do this by myself." His accent grew stronger when he spoke about his connection to the past, almost as pronounced as it had been when we'd been in Kingston. He glanced away as if trying to escape some memory, and then his gaze returned to mine, and his eyes were probing and direct. "Do you know how I feel about you?"

"No."

"You are a constant in my life, and I'm not quite sure what to do about it."

His thoughts reflected my own, the ones I would never say. But I was sure that my eyes gave me away; they always do. I find it hard to hide my feelings, and harder in this case because my feelings toward Basil Dupre were so contradictory. I believed every word he said, yet was never sure he was telling me the truth. I yearned to spend another night with him, yet knew that I should turn him down if he asked me. I didn't entirely trust him, yet would trust him with my life. Our connection was the most baffling and exciting bond I'd ever shared with a man.

I took another sip of my drink, avoiding his eyes and the truth that mine would reveal. "Why don't you tell me what you know about Delmundo Real," I said. "That's why I came."

"Is it really?" he asked, amusement in his eyes.

"So where do you know him from?" I asked, refusing his invitation to seduction.

"Here. There. Places where you least expect to see him. But wherever he goes he brings violence and mayhem into the lives of those who let him near." He was serious now, and his eyes were troubled. "I have known many bad men," he said gravely. "Far more bad than good, if the truth be told."

"I've known my share, too."

"I hope you don't consider me one of them," he said, with a slight, shy smile.

"I wouldn't be here if I did." Basil certainly wasn't "bad" in the sense I meant it. I wasn't sure what he was, but I knew he wasn't that.

"We all have good and bad within us. I have no doubt that I do, too. But you learn to accept all parts of yourself, the good, the bad, the parts you'd like to forget you had. Some of us, of course, tend to always be more good than bad, or at least we think we are." He nodded toward me, obviously teasing me. "And what we consider 'bad' within ourselves always trips us up. Morality is not easily defined, Tamara. More often than not, good and bad is whatever you want to believe, whatever makes you comfortable."

"But morality is easily defined," I quickly disagreed. "There is good and there is bad; there's nothing complicated about it at all. And if you were aiming that crack about being more good than bad at me, I'm not flattered."

"Tamara, sometimes you try to be too *good* for your own good. I know that you don't entirely approve of me. But I've told you that before, too."

"You're right. I don't always approve of you," I said, "but usually I do," I added quickly, softening it with a smile.

"Do you remember what I told you about that man in Jamaica?" He spoke of a man who had nearly killed us both; the memory of that night still crept into my dreams.

"This man, Delmundo Real, is made of the same stuff. Only he is more deadly because he has an angel's face and the wealth to come and go as he pleases. He is an evil thing, and his kind of evil is beyond the realm of morality; that I can easily define. Evil has its own kingdom, and he is one of its princes." I remembered Louella's words about Delmundo Real and an involuntary shudder went through me.

"What do you know about his history?"

"I know not to tangle with him, and if I do and win to make sure he never gets up again."

"So you're his enemy?"

"In a manner of speaking."

"Is he based in Atlantic City?"

"He lives where there is money to be made. Not that much different from me, I guess," he said, with a self-deprecating smile. "But we're not alike," he added quickly.

"Exactly how much money does he make?"

"I don't know, and those who do won't say. In the business that I am in, that is one of the rules."

"And what business is that?" My voice had a sharp edge because I was tired of not knowing.

"Whatever it takes to help me survive," he said, picking up his drink to mark his answer and give me a gentle reminder that I would leave knowing as little about him as when I came. "But nothing I'm involved in will ever touch you, Tamara. I don't make many promises but I made that one to you long ago, do you remember when? It never touches anyone I care about," he added, his eyes admitting that I was one of those people. I wasn't sure if I should be pleased or distressed.

"But what does that mean, Basil? I don't know what danger comes with you, when I should be wary, when I can feel safe."

"You're always safe when you're with me."

"Are you sure about that?"

"I wish I could ease your mind, be who you want me to be, but I can't," he said, his eyes telling me that he meant what he said. "But you know that about me by now, Tamara. You know me with your heart, and that's what you must accept."

"I don't think I can."

"Are you sure?" he asked, changing the mood of the conversation, teasing me when I didn't want to be teased.

"Let's get back to Delmundo Real," I said, putting things back where I was comfortable.

"I warned you about him. Why didn't you listen to me?" His eyes grew troubled again.

"Because my business is *my* own, and it's whatever it will take to help *me* survive," I said, showing him that two could play his game, and the slight fall of his mouth told me he'd gotten my point.

"The word 'Delmundo' means of the world, and 'real' means royal, so he thinks of himself as royalty, which of course he's not," Basil said after a moment. "He came from poverty like the rest of us. Up from nothing, his mind always settling on what others took for granted and what he would never have unless he stole it. You have no idea what it is to be poor as people are in many countries. Americans take it all for granted." He gestured toward the richly appointed room where we sat with mild contempt.

"I've seen my share of poverty, too," I said.

"I know you have," he said, his tone gentler. "But Delmundo Real comes from the kind of poverty you can't imagine. He grew up in the slums of the Dominican Republic. Spent time in Haiti when he was a boy. Killed for the Ton Ton Macoute in their last years and left Haiti a young man with a taste for money and a flair for violence."

"He told me that he acquires things for people. What kind of things does he get?"

"That's what he told you, that he acquires things?" Basil laughed with contempt. "It was a joke, what he said," he added and continued with agitation. "Listen to me, now. Whatever your dealings are with him, abandon them. Leave him alone. Stay out of his way. What do you want from him?"

I sipped my drink, wondering if I should tell him more details about why I was here and why I couldn't just leave, and then decided against it. The Desmonds had paid me well for my skills and discretion, and they had a right to expect both. But Jayne Lucindo's death and how she died was common knowledge, so I told him what I knew about her, and that I had seen her before she was killed. I also told him about Rook.

"I knew plenty like him when I was young," he said. "And you think this boy knows where your runaway is?"

"I'm sure of it."

"He'll never tell you. Loyalty is all kids like that have. He'll never betray her." His eyes left mine. "It frighens me to think my daughter is mixed up with Real. Cruelty and violence are habits that bring him pleasure. The predilections of the men he caters to are beyond comprehension. They're worse than brutes, such men."

"Do you think he's tied up with the murders of these young women?" I lowered my voice, the thought that I had been in the man's presence, completely oblivious to who and what he was, frightening me even now.

"Yes, he's involved somehow, I'm certain of that. But sooner or later they'll find some poor, crazed soul to pin the killings on, and Delmundo

Real will get their message that he or those he works for have gone too far, and the killings will stop. He'll move on to another place. The men who hire him are powerful and their cash makes those who do their bidding invulnerable to the law. They make it possible for him to do his filthy business and never be touched by it."

"Basically then he's nothing but a pimp," I said, my lip turning up in disgust when I said the word as I remembered the last case I'd worked on and the dealings I'd had with a man in that profession.

Basil studied me as if he weren't quite sure what to answer, and then said after a long pause, "He is more than that. He is the hunter who feeds sadistic men their prey. In the last fifteen years, there have been unsolved killings in many cities like the ones that have happened here. Six years ago, in Mexico City, it was young women like here, nameless girls whose deaths went unmourned. It was young boys in Bangkok three years back, and from the favelas of Rio he stole and delivered children under ten. Delmundo Real is found where life is cheaper than shit, and there is no one who cares enough to stop him. It's his first time in the States. I'm surprised he's here."

"So it's not a serial killer?"

"Serial killers are madmen, drifters with no resources. The men who use Delmundo Real's services are neither. He paves their way, and they pay him well. The killings will stop when he is gone, and the evil that comes with him will disappear."

Neither of us spoke for a while. I was lost in thoughts about what he'd just said. He stared out a far window thinking of I'm not sure what. "What were your dealings with him?" I finally said, and his gaze returned to me.

"I rescued a young woman who was important to him. He treats it lightly, still smiles in my face, invites me to his parties when he knows I'm in town, but he would like to cut my throat, and he knows I know it." His gaze lingered on his cognac, and then out the window again, but within his eyes I saw a gleam of ruthlessness I'd never seen before.

"Does he know that Iris is your daughter?"

"I don't know."

"So you must rescue her before he finds out."

"You know me too well," he said, and that look that had been in his eyes a moment ago disappeared. But I hardly knew him at all. "In some ways, I am perplexed by my feelings," he continued after a moment. "I don't understand why I feel so deeply about a girl I've never known and didn't know existed until three weeks ago."

"Because you loved her mother."

"I've loved other women." He paused for a moment. "I was married once for a short time, did you know that?"

"Married? You!" That was one thing I could hardly imagine, Basil Dupre married to anyone, but it was one more thing that told me I knew less of him than I should know.

"I was young enough to believe that love always lasts forever."

"And you don't now?"

"Not the way I thought it did then. We broke up soon after the wedding. I was heartbroken for a while, but it was for the best. There are corners of my life where no one should enter."

"Shining light into those corners is the price you pay when you love someone," I said.

"And what price will I have to pay for loving you?" he asked, not completely seriously, I was sure.

"I've asked myself the same question," I said.

"My relationship with you, Tamara, is unlike any other I've had with a woman." The smile that brightened his face when he said it made me wonder if maybe he was right, if maybe there were indeed deeper levels in what we had together that I was afraid to admit to myself.

I took a cooling sip of my wine to remind myself that making love to a man once does not constitute a serious relationship. And except for the flowers, I hadn't heard from this man since our night together and that usually meant no relationship at all. And those corners that no one should enter could be filled with demons I didn't want to see. Yet each moment we were together etched itself into my soul. I couldn't deny that, either.

"I'm not sure about you, Basil. About us," I said.

"But nothing is sure in life."

"Some things have to be."

"No," he said. "Sometimes that is too much to ask."

We sat for a while longer, saying little until it was time for me to make a decision.

"Will you stay with me tonight?" he asked me.

"No," I said, more quickly than I thought I could. My head told me it was time to go, at war again with my heart. He was disappointed, his eyes clearly showed that, but he wasn't a man to ask a woman twice. We sipped the rest of our drinks in strained conversation and left soon after that. We said little on the drive back to the hotel. When we got to my door, he pulled me into his arms and kissed me. I nearly changed my mind, but then good sense won again—if that was what you could call it—and he walked away.

10

"**F**ool!" was the first word that came into my mind the next morning. It wasn't as if good-looking, sexy men who I was wildly attracted to were pounding down my door. He wouldn't have been the first man I'd made love to simply for the pure pleasure of doing it. Who was I to judge him? Hell, he hadn't asked me to spend the rest of my life with him, just the night.

Disgusted, I got out of bed, stretched out on the floor and did fifty self-punishing stomach crunches. But even as I did them, breathing hard and feeling the flabby muscles around my belly straining to pull themselves into shape, I wondered why the hell I bothered. What was the use? When I'd gotten the chance for adventure I'd tossed it away.

Still irritated, I called room service and barked out an order for coffee and pancakes, trying to cheer myself up with caffeine and carbohydrates. When the food came, I gobbled it down. Still in a bad mood, I pulled out the pad with my notes I'd written two weeks ago and tried to throw myself into my work, which made me feel worse.

It was this frustrating case more than anything else. Although I knew more about some of the particulars—Gabriella Desmond, Rook and even the Desmond family—I was no closer to knowing where Gabriella Desmond was than when I started. Besides that, my little bit of knowledge about Delmundo Real could turn out to be a dangerous thing.

At what point did spending a client's money become wasting it? Had I bitten off more than I could chew? I was just one tired woman working for herself when what the Desmonds really needed was an agency with staff, resources and more expertise. Should I call their lawyer and tell him my misgivings? And there was also the sad possibility—which I was loath to admit—that maybe they'd known all along that I wasn't up to it and that was why they'd hired me in the first place, so Gabriella would stay lost.

Beware.

Basil's warning came back to me with taunting

resonance. If I left the case now, I could make sure that Delmundo Real found out and then he'd know that I definitely wasn't in his business, and I certainly didn't pose a threat. I could go back home to my son where I belonged. If I left now, I'd leave with substantially more money than I had when I started. I could come out ahead.

But there was still Amaretta. If I left without knowing what had become of her, her last frightened look would haunt me for the rest of my days. Had our brief conversation placed her in danger? Would the man who killed Jayne Lucindo kill Amaretta, too? I was certain that Jayne knew Amaretta but she'd been afraid to admit it. How were they tied to Gabriella? I'd have to see it through. I finished my coffee, showered, pulled on some jeans and headed to the casino. Anything for something to do.

The place was as crowded as usual. As I walked through I dropped quarters randomly into slot machines hoping for some random luck. Once or twice, a winning line of fruit and bars danced across the payline and two or three quarters dropped into the tray and rewarded my efforts, but mostly there was nothing, just like the answers in this case. Down to my last bit of change, I pulled the lever one last time and what looked like five dollars in quarters came jangling out. It was a jackpot, more or less, the slot machine's way of tempting me into throwing away more money, but the thrill was gone; I was jaded. I wandered over to the roulette wheel and watched the cool, detached faces of the highrollers as they gambled away more money than I make in a week. Depressed, I headed back to the slots, with the fate of Gabriella Desmond and my missed night with Basil Dupre fighting for space in my mind. Absentmindedly, I began to slide the bulk of my winnings into the first machine I saw, scolding myself as I did so. It was at that moment when I heard a familiar voice boom out from the edge of the casino.

"Girl! Girl! Girl! What are *you* doing down here?" I stopped short. I would know that voice anywhere, but I couldn't believe I was hearing it here. I turned toward the source, nearly knocking over a woman who stood nearby. It was Wyvetta Green, decked out in a sleek silk pants suit the color of money. Her hair, which was always the first thing I noticed, was wrapped in coils around her pretty face and trimmed with gold pins shaped like dollar signs that matched the dollar-sign-shaped earrings in her ears. She had a large straw bag over one arm and a cup brimming with quarters in one hand. She waved to me frantically from across the floor, and I headed toward her, hoping I'd reach her before she screamed out my name. I didn't make it.

"Tamara Hayle! Well, I guess you can get something on anybody. I know I'm a gambling somebody, but I had no idea I'd run into you down here!" When I reached her, she put down her plastic cup and crushed me in her arms. After the last few weeks of Delmundo Real, frustrated searches and murdered young girls, her comforting hug was made to order. "How're you doing, girl?"

"Fine, Wyvetta," I said in as low a voice as I could manage.

"Where's Jamal?"

"Home. Listen, Wyvetta, I'm down here working on a case. Can you tone it down a little? Try to be cool."

"Wyvetta Green is *always* cool!" she said in a huffy voice accompanied by a suck of her teeth. Mildly offended, she turned to a machine nearby and began to shovel quarters into the slots three at a time. I watched without further comment. Within ten minutes, her cup was reduced by half, and she sighed miserably.

"Stop while you're ahead, Wyvetta," I said gently. Ignoring my warning, she rolled her eyes in my direction and slid in some more change. "You got to take a chance every now and then, Tamara. That's what life's about!" I cringed at her words. Without realizing it, she'd hit on what had been on my mind ever since I'd gotten out of bed. "So what you really doing down here? Shacking up with some man?" She paused for a moment to give the machine, and then me, a critical eye.

"I told you, I'm on a case," I said somewhat testily.

She turned and searched my face as if looking for the truth. "Really? You're undercover? Who you supposed to be?"

"Nobody now, just me," I said, realizing that it didn't much matter one way or the other if anybody heard my true identity. Everybody I was trying to hide it from knew already. Feeling sorry for me, Wyvetta grabbed an empty cup from the shelf and poured half her remaining quarters into it and handed the cup to me.

"Here, honey. Try your luck. Go on."

"No, that's okay, Wyvetta, I'm sick of gambling. I just lost about six dollars a minute ago, and I don't want to lose any more."

"Six dollars! That ain't nothing. That's just getting your arm warm."

I handed her back the cup. "No thanks. I'll just watch you for a while, and then I'll be on my way."

She handed it back. "No, girl, take it. Everyone's a gambler at heart. Plus it's easy come, easy go this time. Earl won a thousand bucks over at Trumps last night, and he staked me five hundred this morning to lose wherever I want to. I was winning pretty good until you came over here." She peered at me suspiciously, as if I'd brought bad luck, and then shrugged good-naturedly and slid three more quarters into the slot.

"Earl's a generous man. Thank him for me," I said, finally taking the cup she'd tried to give me. It was impossible to argue with Wyvetta when she had her mind set on something. "I'll pay him back if I win. Where is he anyway?"

"Last time I saw him he was playing the five-dollar slots. Lord knows where he is now. Go on, Tamara, put the money in. Ain't nothing but quarters." She reached into my cup, picked up three quarters, kissed each one and slid them into the slot. As if on cue, a row of bars danced across the payline and a shower of quarters tumbled into the tray.

"Damn," I said, gaping in amazement as I shoveled the winnings into the cup.

"The Lady L is smiling on you this morning," Wyvetta said with a grin.

"It's about time." I picked up a quarter and cautiously slid it into a slot, then watched in disappointment as sundry fruits with no connection to one another appeared on the pay line. Wyvetta shook her head and slid three quarters from her cup into the slot.

"You got to play big to win big. As it is, quarters ain't nothing. We should be playing the five-dollar slots, like Earl," she said with a nod in the direction of the other slot machines. "Fifty quarters ain't nothing but about twelve dollars. Playing five dollars can win you a couple of hundred in the five-dollar slots." A cascade of quarters filled her tray and she scooped them up into her plastic cup. "See that!" She pointed toward the tray. "That's about thirty quarters. Chump change. If we'd been playing five-dollar slots I'd have something." She looked at my bewildered face and cackled. "I'm a gambling nut, ain't I?"

"Nut is the operative word, Wyvetta," I said. "You should take all those quarters you've won and cash them in *now*."

"Easy come, easy go," Wyvetta said with a shrug.

"You're going to wish you had that money tomorrow."

"It's a game, baby, and I'm down here to play it. Gambling is like anything else, if you know how to handle it," she said as she slipped three more quarters into the machine, and then three more in quick succession when nothing came up.

"How long have you been in town?" I asked her.

"Since Thursday. Earl came down to spend some time with his daughter Sandy, and we hit most of the other casinos yesterday afternoon and last night. We'll probably play this here for an hour or so, hit a few more of the casinos, and then drive back sometime late tonight. If one of us hits big, and that will be Earl because he's playing big, we'll get a room somewhere and spend the night. Otherwise, we'll be back in Newark in time to go to church tomorrow morning."

"It would behoove you to save some of that money you're losing and put it in the offering bowl," I said, and the quick twist of Wyvetta's lips told me I'd come off sounding more sanctimonious than I meant to. But then her face softened, as it always did when she offered somebody advice she felt they needed.

"You're starting to sound like an uptight old lady, Tamara. You're worse than some of those straitlaced old biddies who show up at service Sunday mornings. There ain't nothing wrong with taking a few chances and gambling every now and then as long as you don't make a habit of it. You got to grab the good times while they roll, baby. God knows, there's more hard times than most of us can stand in a lifetime. Loosen up. Kick up your feet some!" She did a chorus-girl kick, gave my cheek a pat, then turned back to the slot machine. I thought again about Basil Dupre and decided maybe she was right.

"You thinking what I'm thinking?" she asked, with a glance in my direction.

"I doubt it."

She patted the slot machine as if it were alive. "This here machine is cold. We done milked this one for all it's worth. We got to find us a hot one." She grabbed my arm and ushered me into another section of the casino, pausing occasionally to drop quarters into random machines, then moving on to the next one. We wove our way around the casino, finally parking ourselves in front of a machine that Wyvetta, after having watched it for several minutes, declared to be "hot." The machine bordered the area containing the blackjack tables, and Wyvetta watched those gathered around it and gave a low whistle. "Now that's gambling," she said with undisguised admiration. "It takes balls to sit down with the winners. These folks are some *serious* players."

I had to agree with her about that. The dealer dealt the cards fast and expertly, scarcely giving players a chance to react. Chips in stacks were placed on and removed from the table in smooth, cool motions. Games were swiftly won or lost, and no words, looks or displays of emotion between the players and the dealer were shown or exchanged. I thought about the poker players in Delmundo Real's suite the evening I'd been there. The energy had been the same as here: fear, dread and exhilaration.

There were four players sitting at the table. The one nearest us was a red-faced man dressed in a tailored black suit who had the unfortunate habit of compulsively stroking his toupee, presumably hoping it might bring him luck. Hairdresser that she is, it was too much for Wyvetta. "Let's pray that fool wins. He got to get himself something else to put up top his head besides that rug. I ain't never seen one that looked as ratty as that!" she said with a snort. A small blond woman in a low-cut red dress sat next to the man. On first glance, she appeared to be in her late twenties. But the wrinkles embedded in the leathery skin around her neck and the age spots on her wrinkled, diamond-studded hands cruelly pointed to the truth.

"That's one thing you got to say for the sisters," Wyvetta whispered as she gave the woman a quick once-over. "Only things that show our age are our boobs and our attitude." The third player was a balding black man who smiled and laughed lightly but whose eyes on closer examination held nothing but anger and desperation. Without comment, Wyvetta shook her head then shuddered.

The fourth player was Carver Desmond. His

face was a mask of despair as he watched the dealer place the cards in front of him. It was clear, even in the short period during which we'd been watching him, that he had been losing big. Wyvetta watched him for a few moments and then turned to play her machine. "Can't stand to look no more," she said. "That boy there is in real trouble. I'm surprised they even let him in here to play. Most of the casinos will put the word out on somebody if he's trouble, and that boy is t-r-o-u-b-l-e trouble!"

"Why do you say that?"

"He was over at Carlos, the casino across the street, when we were there, and he got to carrying on something terrible with the guy who was dealing the cards. Jacked the dude up by the shoulders, spit in his face and then all of a sudden the boy started to cry, bawling like a baby. I felt sorry for him. There ain't no need to take a card game that seriously. They were going to call the police, but then they just threw him out. That boy is in deep stew. Ain't nothing going to save him. He's the worst I ever seen." She shoveled her quarters into the slots, following them with three more when nothing happened. "Not as hot as I thought it was," she said.

"What do you mean?"

"Well, when you got a machine that's hot, you

win, Tamara. And there's always something about the feel of it, the vibration—"

"Not the machine, Wyvetta, the kid."

She glanced over her shoulder and then at me, her gaze telling me I'd asked a stupid question. "Anyone who carries on like that boy did last night has obviously got a problem, Tamara. Besides that, look at his eyes," she said. "A game like that where everybody's looking at you, it's not just about the money, it's about showing off. It's about taking the risk in front of folks, like an exhibitionist stripping down to his drawers in a room full of people. The kind of gambling I'm doing here with these slots? Ain't nothing at risk. I can stand in front of this thing all night long, lose all my money, your money, my baby's money and nobody's going to be the wiser. Slots is a chicken game. You can lose your shirt, but don't nobody got to know about it. That's why you get a lot of these little old ladies playing the slots. It's like slamming down gin in the privacy of your kitchen."

"So the ones who are playing cards like that play it for the risk?"

"Not everybody. For some folks it's just fun. Earl plays a little blackjack every now and again but he can let it go. But that boy got the look about him, same look a crack fiend has got or a lush or any other kind of junkie. Look at his eyes, Tamara. The way he holds his body. He can't walk away from it until all his money's gone and they won't let him play no more."

Wyvetta sighed then as if remembering something sad, put in a quarter and was answered for her trouble with ten more.

"Wyvetta, how do you know so much about gamblers?"

"You know, my daddy was a gambling man. He had sense enough to put away the money Mama left us. That's how I got the Biscuit and all," Wyvetta said, referring to Jan's Beauty Biscuit, the beauty salon she owns that she named after her mother. "But Daddy threw away everything else he had on cards and ponies. He was lucky sometimes, I'll give him that, but most of the time he lost it. It's like there's a hole they got to fill that won't let them fill it. For my daddy it was Mama's dying young as she did. I'm older now than she was when she died. Ain't that something?" she said, with a trace of the sadness that often comes into her eyes.

I was struck by how little I knew about Wyvetta's life, about the things that motivated her and how much wisdom and feeling could be found beneath her outlandish hairdos and outrageous clothes. How little did we really know about anyone, I wondered, about the savagery or beauty that lay buried in somebody's heart?

A gasp went up from the blackjack table as somebody lost or won big, and I glanced in Carver Desmond's direction, wondering about the hole that was in him. Had Gabriella's disappearance made it deeper? At that moment, he glanced up at me, and his eyes grew large as his gaze fastened on me. I shifted my body away from Wyvetta, sensing it was best if he didn't know I had run into a friend. I didn't want him calling the Desmonds to tell them I was hanging out, partying and playing the slot machines with their expense money. Wyvetta took the hint.

"Let me get my buns out of here and go look for Earl," she said, her eyes focused on the machine. "I have had enough of these bad boys for today. Good luck with whatever you're doing. See you back in Newark." With a curt nod of farewell, she moved away from me and through the crowd toward the dollar machines. Carver's gaze still rested on me. He played another hand and then got up from the game and came over to where I stood.

Wyvetta was right about him. He looked desperate, and I knew he probably hadn't changed clothes in a couple of days. His eyes were red, too, and he hadn't shaved. I wondered where he was staying and if he'd had anything to eat.

"Don't tell them," he said when he approached me.

"Don't tell who?" I asked, knowing full well who he was talking about.

"My father. Don't tell my father." I wondered what he thought about his stepmother, and why he referred to one person as "them," but I didn't ask him.

"So your father disapproves of your gambling?"

He didn't say anything but seemed hypnotized by something he heard or saw. His general demeanor alarmed me, but maybe it was what I had just learned about him. He stared at me, his eyes blank. I wondered if he could be high on something.

"Carver, how long have you been here?"

"Wednesday." He said the one word in a whisper, so low I could barely hear him. "I came down with my father."

"Is he still here?"

"No."

"Where are you staying?"

He looked lost again, as if he didn't know what I was saying, and the look of desperation in his eyes made me think again about that hole Wyvetta had mentioned. Something I couldn't interpret flickered in his eyes, and I wasn't sure what to make of it. But maybe he was just tired, I decided. He looked as exhausted as I'd ever seen anybody look.

"Come on," I said. "Let me get you something to eat."

He followed me without protest, and we went to one of the small cafes bordering the casino and sat down at a booth as far away from the action as I could find. He stared straight ahead, hardly hearing me when I asked him what he wanted to eat. It was still early so I ordered breakfast food: an omelette, toast, coffee for us both. He jammed the food in his mouth, shoveling it down ferociously, with table manners that would have appalled his proper relatives. When he finished, he polished off three cups of coffee, gulping them down without looking at me, as if unaware of my presence.

"You gambled away all of your money, didn't you?" I tried to take the accusatory edge out of my voice. "And your parents disapprove of your gambling?" He didn't answer me.

"Who was that woman you were talking to?" His voice was nasty, condescending, and I was as surprised by the tone of it as I was by the question itself and the fact that he had noticed Wyvetta. "Were you spending my parents' money?"

Taken aback, I stared him down, not sure who he was trying to be or where he was coming from.

The anger was written not only in his face, but in his entire body, as if the food he'd eaten had given him the strength to be hateful, like his father could be. What had come over him? I wondered.

"What's wrong, Carver?"

"Nothing."

"You have to talk to somebody about the gambling," I said. "You're a compulsive gambler."

"I don't have to answer to you."

"And I don't answer to you," I said. My voice was firm but not mean. "When did it start?"

Something flickered again in his eyes, a dull light, somewhere between despair and rage.

"You have to do something about it," I said as gently as I could.

He looked me straight in the eyes then. "It's too late, now."

"Your parents love you. If you tell them about it, they will get you help, and they have the resources to get you the help that you need."

He stared at me as if I could give him something he needed, and then grabbed my hand from across the table and held it. I hadn't noticed the cuts on his hands before. Some were deep, some shallow, several looked as if they had been inflicted recently. They pointed to self-mutilation, and I wondered if his guilt over his gambling had caused him to do it, the guilt along with his unresolved grief over finding his mother dead by her own hand. His grip was strong. He seemed unaware that he was hurting me.

"Did you say that your father was down here?"

"Don't mention my father again."

"Where is he now?"

"I said don't mention my father again!"

"Why won't you talk about your father?" I said as gently as I could.

"You don't know what happened to me," he said.

"The same thing that happened to me," I said, skipping my question about his father and opening up that old wound again because we shared a common grief different from what most people will ever know. "My brother committed suicide when I was about your age," I said. "I know what that kind of thing does to you. I know how long it takes to heal, but it will heal. Little bits of it at first, so you hardly know they've been touched, and then one day you can finally cry about it and then one day you can talk about it."

His grip grew tighter as I spoke, squeezing my hand. I pulled my hand away from him and rubbed it, bringing the feeling back. A slow smile that puzzled me came over his lips, as if he had played some kind of joke on me and was laughing at me. But grief takes many forms and perhaps this was one of them.

"It's not too late to see someone and talk to a therapist," I said. "Even years later, therapy can help you get through the pain that sometimes seems like it will make your life unbearable. I think your gambling is a way of dealing with your grief."

"You have no idea what it is to be a Desmond," he said. "You don't come from anything so there's no way you could know. You can't know what you have to hold up. Who you always have to be. What would happen if anybody found out about it."

"You don't know what I come from so don't say I come from nothing," I said quietly. "But I think I understand."

"I want to disappear. To make it all go away. To be gone forever and ever, to be nothing. Like my mother did."

I froze when he said those words. "That's not the way," I said. "I know what happened to your mother so soon after your uncle. I know how devastated you must have been." Yet even as I spoke, I wondered if I was taking things too far, wandering into areas where I had no business going. I knew from my own experience that it's easier to talk if somebody meets you halfway. But even these words brought nothing into his eyes. No understanding. No vulnerability. Nothing but emptiness. He stood up abruptly, telling me I had gone somewhere I had no business going.

"I don't have anything in common with you

and your stupid past," he said. "Whatever happened to you can never happen to me."

"Carver, I'm sorry, I didn't mean to—" I stammered, knowing he had reacted as he had because I had stumbled into a space where it was obviously still too tender for a stranger to tread. But before I could finish my apology he'd gone.

I'd blown it with Carver Desmond the same way I'd blown it with Amaretta, and maybe I'd made it worse, raking up the past like I had. Suicide still holds shame for many families, and this was clearly the case for him.

Like my mother did.

His words told me he was dangerously depressed. Like my brother had been. So when I got back to my room, I called the Desmonds' lawyer and spoke to the answering service that said he would be out of town until the following week. I called him at home and left an urgent message for him to return my call. Then, realizing that maybe I shouldn't wait, I called the number I had for Dominique Desmond, leaving a message on her machine that I needed to talk to her as soon as I could. I told her there was an important matter about her daughter's health I wanted to discuss, and that I had talked to Rook, her daughter's boyfriend. I also said I thought that her stepson was in danger of hurting himself.

She didn't return my call until Monday morning, and then she explained in a voice that seemed unnaturally calm that she was glad to hear from me because she had to talk with me, too. So we made an appointment for Thursday morning. I prayed that nothing would happen before then.

11

I met Dominique Desmond on her flagstone terrace. It was hot for the first of April, and we talked about the weather for the first five minutes. Trees, probably planted in my grandmother's day, dotted the lawn that stretched to an elegant fountain and kidney-shaped pool. From where we sat, I could see a white gazebo standing amid clusters of tulips. A wheelbarrow and gardening tools leaned against a tree. It was close to noon, and the gardeners were probably at lunch. Carmelita, a middle-aged woman in a starched maid's uniform whose shy eyes lit up her plain face, placed a china plate filled with star-shaped cookies in front of us and poured iced tea into tall crystal glasses. I tried to imagine how it would feel to be rich and have servants at my beck and call.

My people have always been the ones who responded to the beck and calls: washing the laundry, cleaning the houses, feeding the babies, nursing the sick. My mother did day work back when black women were the only ones doing it, and my father worked in the Sherman Williams paint factory in the area of the city Newark folks call Down Neck. Before they came north seeking the proverbial better life, my grandfather was a carpenter and my grandmother a baker known in three counties for her sweet rolls and fancy cakes. Unfortunately none of her baking skills rubbed off on me. I can't imagine rolling a decent pie crust any more than I can being rich. I'd never look as to the manor born as Dominique Desmond did this morning. Yet there were chips in her smooth finish.

She wore a dressing gown of raw brown silk that made her look hot and sticky on a day as warm as this one, and the long rope of pearls around her slender neck looked heavy and uncomfortable. The two-carat diamond on her left hand had acquired a flamboyant twin on her right: a diamond surrounded by a dozen rubies. My grandma used to say you can tell people born to money by two things: when they wear their jewels and how they treat the help. Dominique failed on both counts.

"You can go now." She dismissed Carmelita with a haughty wave of her bejeweled right hand after she had poured our tea. I caught Carmelita's eye and nodded in silent conspiracy, and her grateful smile thanked me for my acknowledgment. Staring at the lawn as if she were contemplating a stroll, Dominique took a slow, meditative sip of tea, then placed the glass down in front of her, tracing the wet line it left on the table with her beautifully manicured fingernail. "No coasters or napkins. This one won't last long. Servants are so hard to train." She smiled pleasantly in my direction as if I'd actually know, then got to the point. "You mentioned my stepson in your message. What did you want to say?" I was surprised by her question. I'd expected she'd start with Gabriella, not Carver.

She studied me dispassionately, waiting for my response as if she had something else on her mind. I'd picked up my tea but quickly put it down to make my report. "I saw your stepson in Atlantic City last week. I understand your husband was down there as well." If she was surprised by that piece of news her eyes didn't show it, and I continued. "I'm afraid Carver is a compulsive gambler. He seemed deeply depressed. I think you should be concerned. You may want to look into some therapy for him. I haven't found your daughter yet, but I have a very promising lead. I found the young man you mentioned when you hired me, Rook. His real name is Cardell Cummings, and I'm pretty sure I can find him again and convince him to take me to her. I think Gabriella may have taken up with him when she stayed in your place down there last summer. Or maybe on one of the occasions when she stayed with her father. Rook seems to know the area, and is very protective of her. I'm sure she's living with him now. I think she's safe." I didn't mention the pregnancy, deciding to save that piece of news for later in the conversation. After I finished, I waited for her reaction. I wasn't expecting the callous response she gave me.

"I know about Rook, and I'm sure she did run away with him. As for my stepson, he's been depressed from the first day I met him. I understand he's been that way since he found his mother after she'd taken her life," she said as casually as if she were commenting on an allergy to orange juice. She paused for effect, and I had the uncomfortable feeling that she'd rehearsed what she was about to say. "After some consideration, I've decided that I won't be needing your services anymore."

Me and Carmelita.

I settled back in my chair and, with a weary sigh, tried to digest the fact that I'd just been fired.

For want of nothing better to do, I picked up the glass I'd put down earlier and took a sip of tea, but the stuff was so bitter it made my lips pucker. It was all I could do to keep from spitting it out. Was this Dominique's preference or Carmelita's revenge?

"Could I ask you why you've come to this conclusion?" The last client who fired me was a famous radio announcer with a terrible secret, and I suspected now that Dominique Desmond harbored one, too. I wondered if she had told Sam Henderson about her decision.

She drank her nasty tea without answering me and then said, "I appreciate your taking the case, as I told you when you said you would take it, and you will be paid accordingly."

"I hope that I haven't done something to displease you?" I pulled out the old obsequious Tamara Hayle.

"If you're worried about references, I will give you a good one, in exchange for your discretion."

"And that's it?"

"Yes. I'd like you to keep anything you've learned about my daughter confidential. That's all."

"You don't have to worry about my discretion, Mrs. Desmond. All information I obtain while working for a client is always confidential, that goes without saying. If you ask your attorney, Sam—"

She raised her hand to stop me from continuing. "That discretion extends to Mr. Henderson. I'd prefer that you not mention this to him. I'll deal with any questions he has myself."

"I see," I said, and saw more than she thought I did. "Do you plan to hire another detective? Perhaps I can recommend someone who—"

"No. I don't think that will be necessary."

We sat in what might pass as civilized silence for a moment or two and then I asked, "So I assume you've found your daughter?"

"In a manner of speaking, yes."

"In a manner of speaking?"

"I've found a way to get in touch with her, which is why I don't need your services anymore."

"Then you don't know where she is."

She paused for a moment. "No."

"And that doesn't bother you?"

"No."

"Are you concerned about her?"

"No."

"And you're just going to let her go on with her life, stay wherever she is?" I've never been able to keep my mouth closed when I should, and I spoke without thinking about it even though it was none of my business anymore, and I could tell by the way she pursed her lips that she knew it, too. I was surprised when she answered.

"I've made contact with her through a third party. Things are no longer as desperate as they once seemed."

"Is this third person Louella Wallace?"

"Yes," she said with a trace of surprise.

"Does Gabriel know?"

"No. I've asked her not to tell him." So this was another one of Louella's little secrets. By forming an alliance with the hated Dominique, the woman whom her husband still occasionally referred to as his wife, she got back at him.

"Then you give her the money to take to Rook and he gives it to Gabriella."

"I just know I give her the money and she gets it to my daughter. It's easier that way."

"For you or Gabriella?"

She didn't answer me so I asked another question. "So when did things change?"

"Recently."

"And you're not worried about the murders, this serial killer who is taking out her friends? Did you know that Gabriella knew Jayne Lucindo, too? Did you know that she lived with her as recently as the week before she was killed?"

It was clear she was still worried, that was easy enough to read in her face, but her response was studied. "Yes. I know that I hired you because of my daughter's connection with Layne Grimaldi and my concern about her safety, but Gabriella only reached out to those kinds of girls because she didn't have any money, and she has what she needs now. She has severed ties with them. Nothing that touches them will touch her."

"How can you be so sure?"

"I don't have a choice," she said, which was no answer at all.

"But you still haven't seen her yourself to make sure she's okay."

Her gaze shifted from mine. "What do you know?" she asked, her eyes narrowing suspiciously.

"I know that your daughter is seven months pregnant."

A spark of something I couldn't read flickered in her eyes. She turned away from me and stared at the lawn again. Two men, one in his fifties and another years younger, strolled across the lawn. They headed in our general direction, then abruptly turned and walked toward the four-car garage. We watched them walk away, carefree in their slow, ambling rhythm.

"Yes. I know that, too," she finally said, her eyes still on the men. "My daughter told me about her condition."

"So you've spoken to her?"

"Yes, I have."

"When?"

"Right after she left Jayne Lucindo's. Right before the murder."

"Why didn't you tell me?"

"I was too stunned to tell anybody."

"She told you about Rook then?"

"Yes."

I asked very cautiously, "Rook says he's not the father of Gabriella's baby, and I believe him. Do you know who the father could be?"

Her eyes filled with tears, and she took the tea to her lips again so she wouldn't have to look at me, and then she changed her mind and gazed at me as if seeing me for the first time that morning.

"Tell me about yourself, Tamara Hayle," she said, which amazed me because she'd just said she was firing me and it was too late for that kind of question. But I sensed there was something else she needed, something she needed to know before I left, so I indulged her curiosity.

"What would you like to know?"

She shrugged like she wasn't sure herself, and then said, "You seem to be a sensitive woman, like somebody a person could talk to." Her voice relaxed into the slight Southern twang I noticed the first time I saw her, close probably to the way it had been when she walked through the doors of the big house. I knew I was glimpsing a side of her that wasn't born to silk and pearls.

"I've been told that."

"Where were you born?"

"Newark. I grew up in the Hayes Homes. And you?"

"Atlantic City. The projects. Like you."

So we had that in common.

"You said you were a mother, right? A single mother?"

"Yes. I have a son who I'm raising by myself."

"I raised Gabriella by myself, too. After my first husband and I broke up. Before I married Foster. It's hard sometimes, right? To do it by yourself. The money and everything, right?" There was an odd note of desperation in her voice, and I wondered where this was leading but her expression gave nothing away; in fact, her eyes were empty of emotion. I thought about her troubled stepson. I also knew she was lying about the single-mother bit. Gabriel Wallace had said she'd jumped right from his bed into Foster Desmond's, and I suspected she had more to gain from lying about that than he did. I wondered what she thought it would get her.

"Yeah. It's hard sometimes. It can get very tough when those bills start rolling in, when you're the only thing you've got to depend on, when your kid begs for something that everybody else has and you know there's no way in God's green earth you can afford it." I let the truth roll out with a short, quick laugh. There was no need to lie about that part of it or let her know I knew she was.

"Is your son a good boy? I mean, does he drink, do drugs, anything like that?"

"No. Jamal is a very good kid." I told the truth with a sense of pride, but I was still apprehensive. I felt as if she were manipulating me with our shared parenting experience, pulling me somewhere I didn't want to go.

"My own mother was one of these self-sacrificing women. She gave everything she had to me. Everything. She sacrificed her life for me in one way or the other. Always went without so I could have. Funny thing is, I ended up with nothing before I married Foster. For all her sacrifices, I had nothing at all. But I'm not that kind of woman, that kind of mother." She laughed lightly as if a passing thought had struck her as funny. "The last thing my mother said to me before she died was take care of yourself, baby, and that's what I've always done. They say that the task of growing up is to distance yourself from what your mother was, to make sure you're nothing like her. Do you think that's true?"

I searched her eyes for an emotion that wasn't there, which surprised me because when a woman talks about her mother something always comes into her eyes—love, sadness or the trace of some bittersweet memory, like Laura the librarian had in hers when she remembered the things her mother had said. I'd had anger in mine once, but it has cooled through the years. I don't talk about my mother much.

"I'm nothing like mine, so maybe there's some truth to it," I said.

"Do you ever think you've given too much to your kid?"

Was that what she needed to know?

"No."

"I mean, do you feel like you've sacrificed too much? We have our own lives to lead, our own selves to look out for. I mean, maybe sometimes they just have to reap what they sow, right? You've got to let them be what they're going to be, and if they're headed for hell, then you shouldn't let them take you along with them, right?"

"What do you mean?"

"I guess you could say I believe in tough love."

"Well, there's tough and there's *tough*. A lot of how tough you are with a kid depends on how old she or he is," I said. "So it's time for Gabriella to leave the nest, and you're throwing her out

with her pregnant self, right?" I was sick of playing this woman's games and I wanted to know
what had happened between her and her daughter and why she was firing me.

Anger flashed in her eyes, and I was surprised
by its intensity. "I explained to you what kind of
child she is. How wild she is. How up to no
good."

"But she's still your child, and she's having a
child, your grandchild. Don't you think she needs
you?"

*She is my heart, I love her more than I love anything
in this world. She is my heart.*

What had changed? I wondered. Why had she
turned so hard?

"I told you before that I'll give her what she
needs."

"But how do you know what she needs?"

"What does anybody need? Money, of course.
Money to make her own way when it's done, and
she'll have enough for that."

"Make her own way as long as it's away from
you, right?" I didn't expect her to answer my
question but she gave me one anyway.

"I begged her to have an abortion when she told
me. I begged her to get rid of it as quickly as she
could. I told her I'd give her the money for that,
that I would find a doctor who would take care of

it, even if it meant going to another country, even as late as it was . . . as late as it is."

"You asked me before about kids," I said more gently. "You have to really listen to them. Your daughter has made her decision to have this child, for whatever reason, and there's not a hell of a lot you can do about it. You can't force a girl to have an abortion any more than you can force her to raise a child. It's her choice. But you have to let her know that you accept her decision and, finally, her child. It's not the end of the world, it's not—"

"Yes, it is." She interrupted me and the despair in her eyes made me believe that she thought it was. Was it shame? I wondered. Did she actually feel that Gabriella's pregnancy would humiliate her and the Desmonds?

"You do her more harm by showing her you're ashamed. She's not the first teenager to get pregnant and won't be the last. You do her more harm than good by turning her away," I said.

"She won't let me see her. She won't tell me where she is." She cried the words out, and I felt my heart go out to her for a moment, despite the side of her I'd just seen. "She doesn't even trust me that much."

"Why is your daughter so afraid?"

"Dominique? What is she doing here?" Foster Desmond said. My back was to the wide French doors that led to the terrace from the study, and I hadn't heard him come outside. I turned around to face him.

He was dressed for tennis today, white shirt, shoes, socks and sporty tennis sweater trimmed in neat red-and-blue stripes. I remembered the picture I'd seen of his family in the library in Atlantic City, the one in which he was missing. "I thought I asked you to contact us only through our attorney."

"I had an appointment with your wife." His puzzled glance at her told me he knew nothing about it, but then his gaze turned back to me, and his eyes didn't leave my face as he spoke to her.

"I told you from the first this was a bad idea, Dominique. I told you that the only contact I wanted the family to have with any of this was through Sam Henderson." His voice was controlled, but I could hear the anger underneath the surface. Dominique dropped her head in either shame or obedience. "I told you from the first that this wasn't in Gabriella's interest, to involve anyone else like this. It will blow up in our face, in her face. If it gets out, it will follow her for the rest of her life."

Dominique Desmond covered her face with her hands, but she didn't make a sound.

"My wife looks upset. I think you should leave," he said.

I stood up to face him. "Why are you both so afraid?" What my grandma used to call the devil in me wouldn't let it go.

They exchanged quick glances, his more curious than hers, and I realized they were coconspirators in something. I had to know what they were concealing. I thought about Rook then, and the way he had recoiled when I asked if he was the father of Gabriella's child. It was as if the very thought of sexual relations with her repulsed and terrified him. She had obviously told him about her family, and he knew he had to protect her from anyone even remotely connected to them. She had certainly told him the identity of her baby's father. Perhaps his own family had been riddled with pain and betrayal similar to that of the Desmonds. That could be why they'd connected in the first place, why the only one she trusted was him. They shared a common history.

I recalled what Jayne had said about Gabriella's behavior, how secretive she was, how uncomfortable in her own body and how volatile she could be, given to inexplicable fits of anger. Jayne had called her a "Goody Two-Shoes" when it came to sexual involvement. These could be some of the symptoms of an incest victim.

Why hadn't I seen it before?

My gut instincts about Foster Desmond had

been right. The domineering control he'd exerted over his wife he exerted over his daughter, who looked so much like her mother the older she became. I understood now why Dominique wanted me to let it go, why her daughter's presence in the family was the end of her world and why her tears had come so easily when I asked the identity of the father.

When had it started? I wondered. *How long had she let it go on?*

"You got pretty desperate when you found out she was pregnant, didn't you?" I said to him.

"Pregnant?" He looked at me strangely.

"But you can't hide from the law. Even a rich man like you can't hide from a charge of sexual abuse, from rape!" For a moment I was sure he was going to hit me. I could see it in his eyes and the way his body tensed as he forced his hand to stay at his side. I stepped backward, warding off an undelivered blow, cursing to myself for facing him alone but despising him so much I couldn't control myself.

"What the hell are you talking about?"

"You know damn well what I'm talking about. You were looking for her when you went to Atlantic City, weren't you?"

He stared at me for a moment, and then his mouth dropped open with incredulity. "What are you saying? How dare you accuse me of something as disgusting as that!" He spoke so low and his voice was so angry I could barely hear him.

"My accusations are nothing compared to what they'll do to you when the district attorney gets ahold of you!" I lowered my voice, too, making it as menacing as his. "You really are a filthy bastard!"

"Get out of here." His voice had turned into a raspy whisper. "If I ever hear a hint of those lies about me and my daughter, I'll sue you so fast for slandering my name your grandchildren will be paying your debt. I'll wipe you off the face of the earth, Tamara Hayle. Do you hear me?"

"You can do anything you want to me, but there's nothing you can do to touch me." I hurled my words at him, the force of the law on my side.

Dominique stood up and turned to me. "Please go," she said, defeat written on her face. "Don't make him mad. Please, just go."

"If you're not out of this house by the time I get to the phone, I'm calling the police and having you arrested for trespassing."

"Good. And I'll tell them just what's transpired here," I shouted as he headed toward the door. Then I turned to confront his wife.

"Why?" was all I asked her.

"They used to say that the only reason he married me was because he wouldn't have to change the monograms on the linen and silver. D.D. just like his dead wife, Dorothea Desmond, and because I look like I do. I told you what I come from. I'm nothing without what he's given me. I'm nothing at all without him."

"And you sacrificed your daughter over some bullshit like that? You betrayed her so you can be comfortable!" I couldn't hide the outrage, the anger that I could barely control. I recalled Gabriel Wallace's characterization of his wife and his words now rang true in a new and dreadful way. Dominique Desmond was truly an immoral woman, and her home harbored the worst kind of sin imaginable. I understood now the nature of this home that had driven Carver Desmond from it. I understood the depression that crippled him.

"My daughter will be taken care of. She *is* being taken care of. I will see that she gets the money she needs, for everything she needs. I will take care of everything I have to."

"But he is guilty of a crime, and he will end up in jail. You and Gabriella are the victims, not him. There's nothing he can do to you," I pleaded with her to understand, despite my feelings toward her. "He raped your teenage daughter, for Christ's sake!"

Her laugh was bitter and edged with contempt,

but her eyes were filled with tears. "You really don't have any idea, do you?"

"You disgust me," I said, barely able to speak. There were tears in my eyes now, too.

"I disgust myself," she said, "but I've done the only thing I can do."

I left that house as fast as my legs would carry me.

I didn't draw a good breath until I was sitting behind the wheel of the Blue Demon. I sat for a few moments, still too shaken to drive, and then downshifted the car into reverse and haul-assed out of the driveway doing close to forty as I tried to put my thoughts in order. The arrogance that comes with money and privilege never ceases to amaze me. Despite all evidence to the contrary, I knew that Foster Desmond would deny raping his stepdaughter to his dying day. And his wife might deny it, too. The girl had no choice but to run away.

I'd heard of women who, out of weakness and cowardice, continue to live with men who have abused their children. Usually they stay because they are too terrified to change their situation or deal with the truth. They blind themselves, not admitting what they know or sense. In many cases, the man has brutalized them as well, and they are too terrified to leave, afraid for their own lives or that of their children. I also know women, also scared with no resources, who would blow the bastard away, to hell with the consequences, if they found out he was messing around with one of their kids. But in all my years, I've never heard of a woman who would accept her daughter's degradation as payment for her comfort. This was a new one for me, and it made me feel sick and dirty just thinking about it. Yet even Dominique Desmond felt guilty and ashamed, which was why she had shared her feelings with me. But if she'd expected some kind of absolution, she sure as hell didn't get it. There wasn't that much empathy in the world.

I headed for the Garden State Parkway at breakneck speed and then drove south toward the Atlantic City Expressway. It was a two-hour drive back to Atlantic City. As soon as I got back I could check out and make my way back home, and with any luck, I could be back in time for dinner. At least this was all over, and I was richer than I had been a month ago. Much richer. Maybe I'd call Jamal and we'd go out for a late dinner. Red Lobster, of course, he'd like that. I made myself think about Jamal, forced myself to think about the menu at Red Lobster and the food he likes to eat, about the popcorn shrimp he always orders and how he likes to finish up my pie. Maybe I'd invite

Annie to go with us, too. She'd order her usual salad and soup, and then ruin everything by piling on too much blue cheese dressing. I smiled when I thought about that. I thought about stopping to call them and then decided I'd surprise them. I'd walk in the door, smile on my face, cash in my hand, ready to take everybody out. I forced myself to focus on everything but what I'd heard in that house.

The two lanes leading into the city were tight and narrow with no shoulder on either side. There was nothing much to see except for an occasional evergreen and trees, mostly naked with new buds pushing out. It was going on four. Rush hour hadn't started yet, and there weren't many cars heading south. Again, I forced the Desmonds and their daughter out of my mind. I didn't want to get angry again or I'd be too angry to drive. I'd think about it later, when I could do something about it. I was out of it, now, at least for the time being, so I drove hypnotized by the road. I had no idea how long the car had been behind me when it caught my eye.

It was a late-model Lincoln, black and shiny, that would pull up to the rear of my car, as if it were going to pass me, and then slow down again, fall back, then pull up again. It stayed on my back, pulling up, dropping back, pulling up, not allowing other cars to pull between us. Conscious of it now, I slowed down to see if he did, and then drove fast, flooring the pedal. I slowed to a crawl again, observing from my rearview mirror the two cars that slowed behind us, nearly bumping his rear fender. A horn blew twice, then again. Far in the distance, I made out the twirling lights of a state police car, and I put on my hazard lights and pulled to the side. The driver pulled ahead of me, passing quickly. When the cop pulled up to check on me, I told him that my car had overheated. The Lincoln was nowhere to be seen by then, and there was no sense in telling him the truth since I wasn't sure what it was. The cop offered to call for help. I smiled sweetly and told him it wasn't necessary. But I knew that I had been stalked.

12

I've always been able to tuck away my fears and go about my business without so much as a blink or a look behind me. It's something I did when I was a cop—be scared shitless and still kick ass and take names. Maybe I learned it from my brother, who could sell the biggest, loudest woof tickets going while shaking in his shoes. It's something that has always served me well.

I pulled away from the state trooper that afternoon with a look of pure serenity on my face, and by the time I wheeled down the Atlantic City Expressway toward Atlantic City, I'd convinced myself that whoever was behind me was just some dumb somebody having a little fun, singling me out because he felt like bullying a tired little Jetta with his big fancy car. Or maybe he was one of those pain-in-the-ass drivers who try to force you to drive faster by riding your rear fender. Whoever it was had disappeared, or so I told myself, and I didn't have to worry about him. Besides that, when I pulled into the garage I found something else to irritate me. The garage attendant, with a smarmy grin on his face, breezily informed me that there was no more space in the garage (at least not for the Blue Demon), and I'd have to park in an outdoor lot down from the hotel. Grumbling all the way, I parked where I was told and fastened The Club in place on my steering wheel, wondering even as I turned the key who would want the car but me.

I listened for unfamiliar sounds coming from behind me on the way back to the hotel, but except for a bunch of noisy teenagers carrying on foolishness down the block and a woman in high heels walking behind, there was nothing unusual. When the heels came close, I snuck a peek at the walker, a petite, middle-aged brunette more frightened than me. I tossed her a reassuring nod (Tamara Hayle, tough-girl protector) and, determined not to let my paranoia get the better of me, didn't look back again.

But when I got back to my room I realized that driving home was out of the question. My job had officially ended when Dominique Desmond fired me so my room was covered for another day. Why not make the best of it? I reasoned. Maybe it was time to relax a little, take it easy for a change. I decided to treat myself to a last meal, courtesy of the Desmonds, and get something expensive like salmon or steak. Maybe I'd order a movie. Tomorrow I'd be on the road before ten and sitting in my own little house by the time my son got home from school. We could go to Red Lobster then. My life could return to normal.

Up until then, I'd avoided taking even so much as a bag of potato chips out of the minibar in my room, but that night I needed a drink. I filled the Styrofoam ice bucket with ice cubes from the dispenser down the hall and poured most of a mini bottle of Bacardi rum and a diet Coke into a bathroom glass. Without a glance at the notes I'd jotted down over the last month, I tore them up and flushed them down the toilet. I changed into my robe, set the volume low on the TV and settled back on my bed, stockinged feet up, pillow under head and chilled, as my son says.

There's nothing like rum on an empty stomach to put you in a reflective mood and that was what I drifted into. I decided to call Jake on Monday and share what I'd learned about Foster Desmond. He'd tell me the best way to proceed. Foster Desmond deserved to be behind bars, and he would be if I had anything to do about it. I was still puzzled by the vehemence with which he had denied my accusation. He was obviously a man who yelled the loudest when he was wrong. I wondered what threats he'd used to chase Gabriella away, and what he'd try to do to her when she came back. What kind of hell had Gabriella and Carver shared? But I was out of it now. I had my own problems to worry about.

Stay away from mine.

If Basil was right about Delmundo Real, if he was responsible, even indirectly, for the killings, then I should share those suspicions with the police even though they would probably dismiss them because of my source. But maybe my old boss Roscoe DeLorca would be more receptive to my information. He respected my opinion. He also knew powerful people in state law enforcement agencies who would listen to him. And yet there was always the chance that Basil was wrong and the murders were coincidental, just as the police believed. I finished off the little bit of rum in the bottle and began to pack, thoughts of the last few weeks coming and going in my mind. There would always be questions, I realized. I would never know all of the answers. I'd just have to accept that. I'm not sure what impulse made me glance at the television, but when I did, I stopped and sat back down on the bed. The banner that scrolled across the bottom of the screen riveted me to it.

TWO MORE WOMEN MURDERED.

I tried very hard to read it with detachment. I was going home, I reminded myself. I didn't need to be involved anymore. It was over for me. But I knew I had to listen to it, so I turned the television up and tried to hear it as a spectator, one of the thousands of people who had no connection with the case or anybody in it. At least that was what I told myself.

According to the report, both victims had been beaten to death but killed at different times. The younger of the two had been murdered within the last few days. The other woman, who was older, was badly decomposed, and the coroner thought that she had been dead for nearly a month. The older woman had been identified as Livia, last name unknown, a prostitute. The other woman was thought to be a teenage runaway who they believed was new to "the Life." Both bodies had been found out of doors in undisclosed locations.

For the next fifteen minutes, a string of experts and police officials dispassionately discussed the crime, putting their particular spin on it as they tried to reassure the public about the safety of the city. Although they claimed that the lives of all women were valuable, they implied that women who "lived within the confines of the law" would be less likely to meet such a fate. An expert on serial killings warned that prostitutes were the perfect victims for serial killers. They made themselves vulnerable by going to unknown places with strange, possibly violent, men. Peering solemnly into the camera, he warned that the discovery of victims seven and eight meant that the killings might be more widespread than suspected. As he spoke, a chart showing the names of the victims and the dates they were found appeared on the screen.

SPARKLE, LATE ON FRIDAY, NOVEMBER 6, MURDERED EARLY THAT MORNING; DEIDRE, HISTORY OF ADDICTION, MURDERED ON DECEMBER 4; LINDA LAVAL, DAY SHORT OF 18, SUNDAY, JANUARY 3, BEAT TO DEATH ON NEW YEAR'S DAY; JOSEPHINE, FEBRUARY 5 . . .

He stated that law enforcement had begun to suspect that this was a serial killer and that on March 5, Layne Grimaldi's death proved it.

He brought up again what the police had said when they found Jayne Lucindo last Friday—that the time between killings was getting shorter and that the killer was varying how he disposed of the bodies. Although they hadn't determined yet exactly the time of death of the latest victim, the expert said he would "lay money" on it falling around the nineteenth of February, between the murder of Josephine on the fifth of February and Layne Grimaldi the next month.

Disgusted, I snapped it off, sick of everything I'd heard. The only thing I could think of was my last conversation with Jayne, and the sorry legacy her parents left her. Her memory would fade to nothing by the end of next month, just like that of her friend Layne. They had similar names, the friends had died in the same awful manner on the same day of the week. They both knew Gabriella Desmond, Rook and probably Amaretta.

Were all the victims tied to those three or was it only Jayne Lucindo and Layne Grimaldi?

The question taunted me, whirling around in my head with the rum until I felt dizzy. I threw the drink away, lay down on the bed and closed my eyes.

"Let it go. Let it go. Let it go!" I said aloud.

When you're a cop, there's always a point when you have to accept that you'll never find the answer. You won't get the husband who stabbed his wife or the kid who robbed the store or the woman who kidnapped the baby. You've dedicated your life to making wrongs right, but sometimes it just doesn't work that way, and you have

VALERIE WILSON WESLEY

to give it up, and that's hard. I wasn't a cop anymore, but I felt that same frustration now, the same overwhelming anger, the same sense of failure. But there were no answers to be found. And I'd been fired anyway. I had to let it all go. I forced myself to peruse the room service menu, made myself think about going home, about my son.

Amaretta.

I couldn't let it go.

Was she the young unidentified victim, new to "the Life"?

I felt the kind of dread that begins in the marrow of your bones and won't stop gnawing at you. If Amaretta was the last victim, then it was my responsibility to claim her body, and that sense of duty shot through me as strongly as my sense of dread. There would be nobody else who cared enough to do it. She deserved a decent burial. Someone would have to find out if she had next of kin. Somebody had given her those pearl earrings and deserved to know what had happened to her. Maybe it was time for me to go to the police, to share what I knew about Delmundo Real, Layne Grimaldi, Jayne Lucindo and Gabriella Desmond. It was time to lay it all out before there was another victim. I couldn't wait any longer. It had to be tonight.

I was ashamed. I should have gone to the police

232

after the death of Jayne Lucindo, but I'd been too concerned about preserving the Desmonds' confidentiality and my own negative feelings about cops, too concerned about making a buck. If I had gone to them with everything I had, then maybe some scrap of information could have saved this last life.

I sat up on top of the bed, overwhelmed by guilt and a belated sense of responsibility. It wasn't yet ten, but it wasn't too late to make things right. I slipped back into the suit I'd taken off earlier, gargled with Listerine and brushed my teeth—I didn't want to show up at the precinct smelling like rum. I checked the phone book on the night table for the address of the nearest station.

I stopped at the valet desk to call for my car, so focused on my thoughts I'd forgotten I'd parked it in another lot. A sneering attendant reminded me where it was, and I headed toward it, too preoccupied with the grim task ahead of me to be concerned with his attitude.

The walk took longer than I remembered, and I silently cursed the hotel for not offering a closer alternative. There seemed to be fewer lights than I remembered, but I was probably imagining it; the news of these two murders had made me tense and fearful. I finally spotted the roof of the Blue Demon and began to dig through my Kenya bag for my keys, fingering my lipstick, blusher, ball-point pens and wondering how the damn thing always managed to get so cluttered with junk. Keys in hand, I approached my car, then stopped short in stunned disbelief, unable to take another step.

The ruin of what had been the Blue Demon stood before me. The windshield, the windows and all of the mirrors had been smashed and a thousand shards of glass lay inside its devastated interior and on the street. All four tires had been slashed, and the car's carcass rested precariously on its hubcaps. The doors and trunk had been chopped into gaping chunks of tarnished blue steel, and tufts of cotton from the black upholstery and dashboard that had been so meticulously polished by Jamal before I left peeked from the slashes. The steering wheel had been pummeled into the dashboard in a mass of twisted steel and plastic. The radio and tape cassette player along with all my precious cassettes—Miles Davis, Cassandra Wilson, Sarah Vaughan—were strewn around like plastic confetti. A sledgehammer, the instrument of the Demon's destruction, lay on the ground like a proud signature.

I've never fainted before, but I was close to it. Everything spun in a dizzying mix of sights and sounds: the sparkling glass, the small group of teenagers gawking at the wreck, the solitary light that shone from a post on a corner of the lot. I walked toward what was left of my car in a daze, my step unsteady.

"Damn, lady, you sure pissed *somebody* off!" cracked one of the teens, trying to be funny.

"Did you see who did this?" I asked him, but my throat was so tight with emotion, I wasn't sure if any words came out. For a moment I thought I was going to cry and prayed, *Please Lord, don't let me bawl in front of these kids.*

"Naw, baby. Ain't nobody seen a thing, not a goddamn thing," one of the older boys mumbled in a manner that told me they had probably seen everything but were scared to admit it.

"You okay, lady?" another kid asked. He had a kind voice that reminded me of my son's.

"I'm okay. I'm fine." I was unsure but said it anyway. I made my way over to examine my car.

"You gonna call the cops? You should call the cops!" one of the kids suggested. I was too stunned to think that far ahead. I touched the car's hood as if it had been alive.

"Hope you got insurance!" one of the older boys said, and the group began to snicker among themselves. I hardly heard them.

I reminded myself that the Blue Demon was just a car, nothing but steel, plastic and rubber tires, but it had represented much more to me and Jamal. It had been almost a member of our family, albeit a noisy, cranky, wheezy one. Jamal constantly complained about its appearance and general condition, claiming that its snorts and bangs were the bane of his teenage existence. He begged me so often to buy or lease a new vehicle, I simply closed my ears whenever the word "car" was mentioned on TV or the radio. The Blue Demon's very nickname had been sarcastically given to it by Jamal in a fit of pique.

The Demon was rusty and old and took forever to start on cold mornings—and often on warm ones. How often had I parked it far from my destination to avoid the embarrassment of claiming it? How often had the depressing sight of it been a sad reminder that if one's car was an indication of success, I was so far down on the scale I couldn't be read. But the car was mine. I'd bought it with my own hard-earned money and loved it in that proud, protective way one grows to love a material object.

It had seen me through many a dangerous scrape, holding its own against cars half its age and twice its horsepower. It had adapted itself to humiliating exterior changes made necessary by my paltry bank count. Yet the radio continued to play despite the substitution of a clothes hanger for its antenna; the muffler still worked despite being supported by the hanger's twin; the rust spots on its hood hadn't gotten any bigger despite weathering many a rainstorm and snowstorm. It had performed its job, and it had performed it well.

I brushed the shattered glass from its hood and interior with a newspaper I picked up off the ground, and slid into the driver's seat for the last time. How often had I sat here, collecting my thoughts, jotting down notes, recording somebody's secret vices. I patted what was left of the steering wheel. My chin dropped to my chest.

"Tamara." Basil Dupre was suddenly behind me. I gazed in the direction of his voice, hardly seeing him.

"Now there go some wheels. Hey, Shorty, you better leave that piece of junk where it's at and get into *that!*" one of the teenagers commented from the sidelines as he checked out Basil's car. Basil threw him a warning glance, and the group scattered.

"Come on," he said, taking my hand and trying to help me out from behind the Demon's demolished interior. When I didn't budge, he stood back and shook his head solemnly and then went to the sledgehammer, picked it up and put it back down.

"Who could have done this?" I asked again. The

Demon had only been a car, but the violence inflicted upon it was overwhelming.

"Who do you think? Have you heard from him again?"

"No. Not since I saw you."

"You never told me what he said to you the night that we were together. What frightened you so?"

"He told me to stay away from what was his," I said, turning away from the steering wheel to gaze at him. I could see the alarm that was in his eyes. "To quote him exactly, he said to stay away from *mine*."

"This is his warning." He nodded toward my car. "He is saying if he will do this to steel, imagine what he will do to flesh. Come on." He took my hand. "Come, let's go." I climbed out of the car and glanced back for one last look. "It's a car, Tamara, not your blood and bones. You can buy another. Come." Basil's smile was like that of a parent patiently urging a stubborn kid to put down a broken toy. He called the police on his cell phone to report what had happened, and when two officers came I made a report, leaving out any mention of who I thought was responsible.

"These damn kids, they're capable of vandalizing anything," one of the cops muttered under his breath as he looked over the wreck of my car. He took down all the information that was needed and gave me a number to call after I spoke to my insurance company, then, still shaking his head in disgust, he and his partner drove away.

Basil and I left, too. As we drove away, the practical problems that came with the loss of my car began to occur to me, questions about insurance— thank God it was paid—how I would get home tomorrow and what I would tell Jamal. I knew I wouldn't get much insurance money, most of the down payment for a new car would have to come from the money I'd earned on this case, money I'd counted on putting in the bank. Every time I took a step forward I ended up dropping two steps back. The loss of my car was the last thing I needed. I gazed out the window looking at nothing. After a while I glanced at Basil. He hadn't spoken at all, and he drove fast, staring straight ahead; it was impossible to read his thoughts.

"How did you know where to find me?" I asked.

"A parking attendant in your hotel told me." His long beautiful fingers grasped the steering wheel tightly, his fingers taut. I'd been so upset about the loss of the car I hadn't noticed how tense he was. "I needed to tell you something."

"What happened?" He didn't say anything; he just continued to drive, holding the wheel as if it had a life of its own. "My daughter is dead," he said finally. He showed no emotion, his voice toneless.

"They found two more women and my daughter was one of them, the young one they couldn't identify, the one they kept saying hadn't been in the Life for long. Something told me it was her; maybe the spirit of her mother. I went to the cops, asked to view the body as a possible next of kin and recognized her at once, saw her mother's face in what was left of hers. Iris." When he said her name a catch in his voice softened it and brought tears to my eyes.

"Her death was meant to be a warning to me," he said quietly, still gazing straight ahead. "He meant to teach me a lesson. He found out who she was. He killed her to show me that he hasn't forgotten. Her death is my fault, Tamara."

His words, spoken almost in a whisper, came from the bottom of his heart and stirred mine. "There is no way he could know that," I said as convincingly as I could, but we both knew it wasn't the truth. But another question, a far more frightening, selfish one, had entered my mind. Did Delmundo Real know of *our* connection? He took his eyes off the road for an instant, enough time to glance at me as he spoke.

"You know what I promised you," he said as if it were a secret between us. "My troubles will never touch you."

"But promises can't always be kept." I was worried and didn't try to hide it.

"The ones that I make always can," he said with a finality meant to put an end to my concern, and I decided there was no use in pushing it anyway. There was nothing either of us could do about it, and I was tired of being afraid. "What do you want to do now?" he asked after we'd driven awhile longer.

We were miles from the city by then and the road lay straight and narrow ahead of us.

"I want to make sure my son is okay," I said. Basil's glance told me he understood and he nodded toward his car phone. I called Annie's house, my voice carefree when I spoke to Jamal, but grave when I talked to her. I explained what had happened to the Blue Demon, and without any suggestion from me, she promised to take Jamal to visit her cousin in Connecticut until I returned home, and then together we could figure out what to do next. The sound of her voice comforted me, and I felt better, as if everything might turn out all right.

"Your best friend," he said when I hung up. "Tell me about her." So I did, nonstop for the next fifteen minutes, about our girlhood, misadventures and anything else I could think of to take both of our minds off the things that had happened.

"Have you told her about me?" he asked with surprising shyness.

"The little I know."

"You say you know nothing about me. I know nothing about you, except that you were the only person I wanted to see when I found my daughter." He was serious now, stating it with no hint of flirtation or flattery, simply as a truth, and I accepted it as that.

"Where do you want me to take you?" He gave me a sidelong glance. It was the same question he'd asked me last week, the last time I'd seen him. I thought about the wreck of my car and the threat of Delmundo Real, and I knew there was no way in hell I could face the loneliness and terror of that hotel room again. There was nobody but him that I wanted to be with, and I told him so. We drove to my hotel and I picked up a few things, and we returned to the inn where we'd had our drink the Friday before.

His room was on the top floor, and I could see the black cloudless sky through the skylights in the ceiling. A mix of pillows in shades of maroon, cream and brown were scattered on the four-poster bed. It was a charming and inviting room made more appealing by its small, elegant touches: the silver candlesticks on the nightstand, the oblong Oriental rug that caught the reds in the bed linens, the small lamp that spread a soft, sensual glow in every corner. Basil smiled when he saw the delight in my face.

"This is where I stay when I come to Atlantic City, never at the hotels." He took off his coat and hung it in the closet. "It's quiet here, takes me away from the madness and noise. It eases my mind, as you do, Tamara."

It was a place designed for a restless spirit that could never be tied to one place. Basil lived in many different cities, I knew that much about him. He'd been in London for a while, years ago in Newark, in Kingston and in Toronto. My roots run deep. I could never live far from Newark where they are planted, and my history and those I've lost cling to me no matter where I am—shadowing my dreams and walking in my present. But Basil was different, which had always puzzled and disturbed me.

"Where do you live, Basil? Really live," I asked him. We sat on a small couch not far from the bed. Sex offers its own immediate comfort but neither of us was ready for that yet. I needed a different kind of understanding between us, separate from the passion that had brought us together before.

"Each city I live in holds magic for me," he said, offering an explanation that I didn't know I needed until he gave it. "London is Brixton, which has its own rhythm and color that take me back home. It's the energy in New York, it grabs me the moment my feet touch the sidewalk. It feeds me, keeps me engaged in life, and alert. I started out in Newark and learned how to make big money there. I met you there," he added, which made me smile. "Kingston I love simply because it's home. I'll go to Jamaica to die, I'm sure of that. I love the excitement of my life, Tamara, the unpredictability, the challenges and dangers I must overcome to stay alive."

Then his eyes suddenly filled with the sorrow I'd seen earlier. "But I must ask myself if I've made the right choices. My daughter would be alive if I had lived my life differently."

I remembered that morning with Delmundo Real when I had sensed that the young woman who had come through the door might be Basil's daughter. Life is always filled with ifs, possibilities, I reminded him of that.

"I don't think there's anything you could have done," I said as much to myself as to him.

"I've made decisions I regret and mistakes I am sorry for. I've done things for which I'm sure I'll burn in hell one day," he said quietly.

"We all have." I didn't like to think about the mistakes and wrong decisions I'd made. Could I have saved her life?

"Yet I've learned to accept my life for what it is, with all of its insanity and recklessness. You can never second-guess yourself, can you? You make the choices you make and live the life you've chosen."

Remembering my conversation with my son, I returned his sad smile with one of understanding. I could no more be the hairdresser or waitress Jamal wanted me to become than Basil could be the kind of man who would fit comfortably into my life. He would never be Jake Richards, the righteous, upstanding, good-provider kind of brother your mama prays you'll marry. Basil Dupre was who he was, take him or leave him, that was the choice.

But in so many ways, I was the same as he. I'd made the same decisions, craved the thrill of my life with its danger and unpredictability. We were more alike than I wanted to admit, and I didn't have the right to judge him or expect him to become my fantasy of what a "good man" should be.

His first kisses were tender, lingering on my lips, caressing my throat and chin gently as if asking permission to go further, which I quickly gave. I was swept into the moment—his lips on my throat, the touch of his hands as they stroked my body, the lingering fragrance of his cologne. I was amazed yet again how easily I was seduced by him, how quickly his touch could excite me, awakening feelings that I'd forgotten.

We undressed quickly and without speaking,

shedding our clothes into a heap on the floor beside the bed. It was only after our bodies touched, the cool silkiness of the sheets unfolding on top and around us that I realized how much I needed him, how good it felt to touch him again. My feelings for him have always stretched beyond words, thoughts or reason—beyond the boundaries that tie me to most men. And that was why I was so wary; there was no stepping back once we embraced.

My body responded to his touch as if we'd been apart for only hours, as if I'd left him only days before. I touched the jagged scar on his left shoulder, delivered, he'd told me once, by a jealous woman in a fit of rage, and which I had to admit to myself I could understand. His body felt the same as I remembered it, only stronger, more muscular, more sure of itself. He ran his lips and fingers over every part of me, arousing me as I hadn't been since he touched me last, in ways I'd forgotten I could be.

We stopped for a moment as he searched the drawer in the nightstand beside the bed for a condom. My mind snapped back to the last time we'd made love and to the gun I'd found in his nightstand drawer that had saved both our lives. I wondered if he still kept one there, subtly intruding into our passion with its brutal presence. But he kissed me again, and it didn't matter one way or the other.

We made love with a familiarity and sense of discovery that I couldn't remember experiencing with another man. I was lost in the power of it, and I knew that if we were together a thousand times each would be like the first. It was foolish for me to think I could fight the strength of our attraction. I fell asleep in his arms, aware only of how close he was to me.

A dream woke me at dawn. I sat in the passenger's seat of the Demon next to a young woman driver. The car was being battered brutally by some invisible force, and each blow drew us closer and terrified us more. Basil stirred in his sleep and pulled me close to him, and I felt protected and safe. I could see a hint of the day to come through the skylights, and I made myself remember last night and how good we'd been together. But unfinished business, troubling and threatening, loomed in my mind.

13

After I left Basil, I rented a car and drove to the hotel. There was just enough time left to check out and try to make it home before that dinner with Jamal I'd promised myself. The parking attendant culpable in the demise of the Blue Demon was nowhere to be seen, and none of the other attendants would look me in the eye. I considered badgering some poor soul into telling me the truth about what had happened to my car but good sense and healthy paranoia got the better of me. It was too late to do anything but bitch. I stopped by the front desk to make sure that my hotel bills had been paid by the Desmonds and there wouldn't be any drama when I finally checked out.

"Everything has been *well* taken care of, Ms. Hayle," the front-desk clerk said with a fawning grin and just enough groveling to show that he knew how important my sponsor was. As I turned to walk away, he leaned toward me confidentially and whispered, "By the way, there's somebody here to see you. Your daughter."

"Daughter?"

"That's what she said. I guess she wanted to surprise you. She came in last night and asked to be taken to your room, but of course we couldn't let her in without your permission, so we put her up in a single room that became available. I took the liberty of adding it to your bill. I hope you don't mind."

"Of course I mind. I don't have a daughter!"

"Well, that's what the girl told me. See that teenager sitting over there." He nodded toward a semicircle of small couches in a far corner of the lobby. "Maybe you should go over and get it straight." He turned back to his work with a sulky attitude that said it was my problem and not his. I walked to where the girl was sitting.

She was sprawled out on the brown tweed couch. Her legs were stretched straight out in front of her and she bopped her head to music coming from the earphones plugged into her ears; her eyes were closed. Her soft natural hair was pulled into two fluffy Afro-puffs that were fastened on the sides of her head by red glass balls. She wore a white T-shirt, oversized gray overalls and gray-and-white sneakers, one of which tapped out the same rhythm as her head. An overstuffed black backpack lay on the floor beside her. She opened her eyes when I sat down beside her, snatched off her earphones and dropped them into her lap. If it hadn't been for the pearl earrings in her ears, I wouldn't have recognized her.

"Amaretta!"

"You remembered!" She gave me a wide grin. "So where you been, Ms. Tamara Hayle! I been waiting since twelve-thirty last night!" The way she emphasized "Ms. Tamara Hayle" told me that she was trying to make a point. I wasn't sure how she'd found out my real name, but I was so glad to see her I didn't want to press her about it, not yet anyway.

"How did you get here?"

"Walked through the door."

"Well, you've certainly had a change of style."

"Like it?" She gazed down at her coveralls with a demure smile. "Figured I'd leave this dumb-ass place wearing the same dumb-ass shit I had on when I came." She shook her Afro-puffed head in my direction. "You thought that hair was real, didn't you? I paid big money for that weave."

"Something must have scared you bad for you to cut it all off, huh?"

She flinched and dropped her gaze. "I just got tired of it." She was lying, but I let it go.

"Thank God you're okay. I was worried about you."

"How come you were worried?" She was puzzled but pleased.

"You remind me of somebody I knew a long time ago."

"Who?"

"A kid about your age. Impulsive, hardheaded, tough, who always thought she was grown. But good luck, a big brother and her grandmama's prayers helped her make it into adulthood."

"Hope you don't mind me telling them I'm your daughter. You got a kid, right?"

"Yeah. A son. But it's okay."

"Can we go to your room and talk? You don't know what's going to come strolling through this lobby." It was clear she was still frightened. We went to my room, and when we got there she said she was hungry, so I called room service and ordered her some breakfast. I also called the front desk and told them I'd be checking out later than I thought. She greedily went through a stack of pancakes, sausage, bacon, eggs and two glasses of orange juice like it was the best meal she'd ever had. When she was finished, she stretched like she was getting ready to work out, then flopped down on the bed.

"It's time for me to leave town," she said as she picked up the remote from the top of the TV and aimlessly changed channels. "I got to get back to Atlanta." She closed her eyes. "Wake me up in an hour so I can get that bus, okay?"

"Hold on, sweetie, we've got some things to get straight first," I said, giving her shoulder a gentle shake.

"Like what?"

"Like last time I saw you you were heading into a bedroom with Delmundo Real," I said, for which I got a smirk and guttural laugh. Then she sat up and turned serious. "You know what you told me at that party?"

"No. Tell me. I don't remember."

"You said I was too young and pretty to be hanging around a place like that. Remember you said that?"

"Yeah, I do. And it's true."

"After you said that I figured you were right so I called my big brother Vernon and told him I was coming home, and that's where I'm heading, back to Atlanta, G.A. I came by here because I was hoping you'd lend me some money, and I needed somewhere to hang out until the bus came, too, and you were nice to me and shit so I figured you might help me out. I'll send the cash back to you when I get back home. That's all." She talked fast, running her words together as if she didn't give a damn one way or the other, but the look in her eyes told me how desperate she was.

"You don't have to worry about sending the money back, Amaretta," I said. "Just knowing that you want to go back home is payment enough. But we have to talk first."

"I ain't got nothing to say." She poked out her lip.

"I need to understand everything that's gone down in the last few weeks, everything that you've seen, and I need to know it now," I said.

"I ain't seen nothing."

"We both know that's a lie."

"Why you need to know?"

"I can't leave Atlantic City without some answers." I had to know the whys and wheres of what had happened because of the grief in Basil's eyes and the fear in my own whenever I thought about Delmundo Real, and because I knew that whoever had been banging on the side of the car in my dream was still out there. There were too many strings still dangling. I had to find out as much as I could for my own safety as well as for hers. That was my unfinished business. She stared at the cartoons that had come on the TV screen without saying anything. I thought about all those Saturdays I'd watched these same shows with Jamal. Even though they were nearly the same age, he would never be as old or act as young as this. She glanced at me out of the corner of her eye.

"So you'll give me the money if I talk? All I need is eighty-four dollars, that will get me a one-way ticket on the Greyhound bus." I took ninety dollars out of my bag and gave it to her. She jammed it into a pocket on her backpack and zipped it closed.

"Thanks."

"I'll take you to the station, too, but I want to talk first. That's important." She glanced around the room again, her gaze going toward the door. I got up, put the double lock on and sat back down. "You're safe here," I said. "Nobody will hurt you as long as you're with me."

"You got a gun?"

"No. I hate guns so I don't travel with them."

"Jayne said you were a private eye. What kind of private eye are you without no gun?"

"One tough enough to protect you if you need it," I said.

She started playing with the remote again. "I just want to get the hell out of here as soon as you can take me."

"So Jayne Lucindo told you who I was?" She put the remote down, and I picked it back up and turned down the volume.

"Yeah. She called me after you came by her

place. Said some lady private investigator named Tamara Hayle gave her beaucoup bucks to tell her where Gabriella was. I asked her what you looked like and when she told me, I knew it was you."

"So you were friends with all three of them, Layne, Jayne and Gabriella, right?"

"Yeah."

How ironic, I thought, that after all these weeks of frustration and discouragement, I was finally getting the answer I'd been looking for about Gabriella from the first person I'd asked. "Where is Gabriella now and is she okay?"

"Gabriella is fine with her big old fat self," Armaretta said with a playful grin.

"So she's living with Rook?"

"Yeah, who else. How do you know about him?"

"Where are they living?"

"About fifteen minutes from here. She doesn't have a phone." She wrote down an address on the back of the room service menu and handed it to me, and I stuffed it into my bag so I wouldn't forget it. "You got to promise me something, though."

"What?"

"If you see Rook, don't tell him you got the address from me. I don't want him going off again on me like he did before. I can't stand nobody calling me out my name using a lot of foul-ass language." She pursed her lips, and I smiled despite myself. "I ran into him downstairs in the casino while I was waiting for you, and he cursed me out just because I tried to do something nice for Gabriella." She glanced at the clock and frowned. "We got to go soon. My bus leaves at noon, and my brother is going to pick me up at six forty-five tomorrow morning."

"Tell me why you came to Atlantic City in the first place, and then what you know about your friends, including Gabriella, and everything you know about Delmundo Real," I said.

"When can we leave for the bus? I told you that bus leaves at noon, and I got to buy my ticket, too. So I got to leave myself enough time for that. Now that I've decided to go I don't want nothing to keep me from getting on that bus." She was worried now, and uncomfortable. She picked up the remote again and started switching channels.

"We'll leave here in half an hour. That should give you enough time." She gave me a skeptical look, took a sip of water and then, because she didn't have a choice, began to talk.

"I didn't like the way my brother was treating me. He's eight years older than me, but he tried to out-mama my mama, even though that's not even his job. That was my aunt's job before she died, that was why I left."

"Where is your mother?"

She laughed contemptuously, and the sound of it let me know my question wasn't funny. "Still on the pipe, if you know what I mean." It took considerable restraint to hide my reaction to what she'd just said.

"So your aunt raised you after your mother became addicted to cocaine?"

"Yeah. Till my aunt died last year, and then my smart-ass brother Vernon started thinking he was the boss of me, and that was why I left. Got tired of him telling me when to come home and who I should see and where I should go, so I saved up my money and I got on a Greyhound coming here."

She started switching the channels with the remote again, and I let her do it for a while without saying anything.

"How long have you been here?"

"Since August. It was hot then. Summertime. I used to sleep under the boardwalk with a bunch of other kids. We'd watch the stars, smoke us some weed, wash ourselves in the ocean. We had ourselves a ball. Sometimes one of us would find money or credits in the machines, and we'd party all night.

"That was how I met Rook. He brought Gabriella down around November, and I met her. By then the weather was cold," she said with a shrug, still playing with the remote. "I had to come inside."

"And when you came inside, you had to do things you didn't want to do so you could eat?" I asked as gently as I could, and the way she avoided my eyes told me I was right, but then she gave another quick, careless shrug to show she didn't give a damn about that, either.

"I figured my mama did it. I knew that because I'd seen her do it. Didn't seem to be too much to it as long as the men treated you okay and if you didn't think about it. My auntie said that her habit was what made her do it, but I figured it was good enough for her so it was good enough for me, too. You do what you got to do. But it didn't work out too tough."

"You didn't think you could go back home?"

"I tried to call my brother a couple of times, but he didn't pay the bill and the phone was off. I thought about writing him, but I was living on the street by then or with Del, and what was I going to put on the letter as a return address—Miss Amaretta Jones, care of the boardwalk? Amaretta Jones, care of the Sultan's Lair? I didn't have an address." She took a spoon and filled it with syrup from the packet that had come with the pancakes and dribbled it on the tip of her tongue, then licked her lips. "When I finally got an address, I didn't give a damn one way or the other anymore."

"So tell me when you met the others, Jayne and Layne."

"Jayne and Layne were tight from before. They were always together. Everybody thought they were sisters at first, they looked so much alike. Layne was white but she always had a tan so she really looked like she was light-skinned or Hispanic or something like that. They both had real pretty hair, too. They used to wear it the same way, too. Hanging straight down their back in this old-fashioned way, like one of them actresses you see in old movies. I met them on the boardwalk, and then they met Gabriella and we all kind of looked out for her when Rook wasn't around. She said she was running from somebody but she wouldn't say who it was."

Amaretta picked up the water, drank it and then went over to the minibar and went through it. "They don't got no amaretto, do they?"

"No. Take a soda. Who was Gabriella running from?" I asked, even though I thought I knew.

She shrugged again. "Hell if I know. Gabriella never says nothing to nobody. She wouldn't even tell anybody who gave her that baby. She talked to

Rook, that was about all. She probably told him. We always teased her about it, told her she was like the Virgin Mary and shit because she wouldn't do nothing with nobody. She said she was going to have it because she didn't have the right to kill it. I guess she thought she and Rook was going to raise it together. Dreamland, right?"

"And she didn't want her people to know where she was?"

"That's why me and Gabriella fell out the first time. I called her mother and told her where she was. I thought the lady needed to know, and Gabriella got mad as hell. And then Layne was killed after that."

"So you were the person who called Dominique Desmond?"

"I called her once where they lived upstate, then left another message for her at this address she gave me down here. I still don't know why Gabriella got so mad about it." Amaretta shook her head as if she were still puzzled. "Gabriella didn't talk to me again until there was nobody else to talk to, after Layne and Jayne. She didn't trust no damn body after that. Only Rook. I think she was afraid somebody would follow her and shit. Everything changed after Jayne died. Everything."

"Tell me about that, Amaretta."

She shifted uncomfortably on the bed for a

while, and then spoke with her eyes pinned to the water glass she had picked up then put back down on the table, and I thought about Jayne and how afraid she'd been the day we'd talked.

How far did the arms of Delmundo Real reach?

"When Layne was killed we just thought it was somebody she knew, some crazy man who had it in for her, but with Jayne, everybody knew something else was going on. Somebody was after her, and he might get us, too." She glanced at me, then dropped her gaze, and I saw the same fear that had been in her eyes that first night.

"Did any of you think of going to the police?" I asked, even though I knew the answer. If a responsible, law-abiding citizen like myself dreaded involving the police then these girls certainly did. The cops would be the last people any of them would want to talk to.

"Jayne wanted to go to the police, but me and Gabriella told her not to do it. Gabriella didn't want anyone to find her. I couldn't go because I was working for Del.

"We were so close for a while, the four of us, like family, all hanging together, going places, joking around. We even dressed alike some of the time." She smiled if she were remembering those times. "Then things started getting fucked up. First Layne, and then Jayne and then . . ." Her voice trailed off.

Like Josie and the Pussycats, I thought as I recalled that Jayne Lucindo had mentioned that old TV show without acknowledging who the fourth girl, the last Pussycat, had been.

"What was it like working for Delmundo Real?" The quick twitch of her shoulders told me more than any words could. She had learned to lie very well, and she did it now with little effort. But I could still see the truth of her experiences in the movement of her body.

"It was fine. Okay," she said with the shrug that marked nearly every remark she'd made this morning. She could talk about her girlfriends, and even about her mother and the pipe and her aunt's death and her anger at her brother, but she was still so shaken by the events of the last few weeks that even now, sitting in the safety of my room, she was still afraid. She was on her way home, and she wasn't taking any chances. I asked her the obvious.

"Are you afraid to talk?"

"No," she said with forced bravado. But her quick response told me how to interview her now: take every "no" for "yes" and each denial for an affirmation.

"You're still afraid of Delmundo Real, aren't you?"

"No!" She dismissed my question with a jaunty toss of her head that didn't impress me. "I'm not scared of nobody."

"Do you think he had something to do with the murders of those women?"

Careless shrug. Eyes big with fake innocence. "How could he? He wasn't nowhere around them."

"And you're afraid that he thinks you know more than you do?"

"I don't know nothing about Del except that he treated me nice." She picked up the empty water glass and brought it to her lips, but her hand was trembling.

"And you knew Iris, too, didn't you?"

"Who?" Her eyes were the biggest they'd gotten.

"And you got to be friends, right?"

"I don't know about nothing named Iris except a flower."

"And when she was murdered, that scared the hell out of you because you knew that you could be next. And that is why you're here, isn't that the truth?"

"No! I just want to get the fuck out of this place."

"Who was responsible?"

"It's going on eleven-fifteen. I got to get on the damn bus," she said.

"If we go to the police they will protect you. I'll see to that. If you hold this man's secrets and—"

There was no fear or timidity in her manner now. Her eyes were narrowed and her voice shrill as she spat out the truth as she knew it.

"They ain't going to do shit!" she said. "I even seen some of them motherfuckers up there partying like the rest of them. I'll take my goddamn chances by myself. Back in Atlanta."

For the next fifteen minutes, I tried to convince her to do otherwise. I told her I'd been a police officer and I knew many good ones who were strong and honorable and would give their lives to protect her. I told her about my former boss, Captain DeLorca, and about my brother Johnny and what a good cop he'd been. I begged her to come back to Newark with me and trust me enough to find somebody who would listen to everything she knew and make sure she was protected. She wasn't hearing it. Finally I confronted her with the cold reality of how I was sure everything would eventually play out.

"Delmundo is rich," I said. "He knows a lot of powerful, rich people who will do things for him, and if he thinks you're a threat to him or his business, it will take him no time at all to find you. And you will be a threat because you no longer work for him. Once he finds you, what do you think he'll do to you? You're just one skinny little sixteen-year-old kid against a very big and very evil man."

"Seventeen," she corrected me. "I turned seventeen two weeks ago, and I don't know nothing about Delmundo Real being evil and it's time for me to catch that bus."

I wasn't about to give up. "Think about your friends," I said. "Think about how he or somebody close to him beat those girls to death. Beat them, and then shot them in their faces. What kind of craziness is that? Do it for them, Amaretta, for Layne and Jayne and Iris."

She didn't say anything for nearly five minutes, during which time she slowly finished off a bag of potato chips and a Coke she'd gotten from the minibar and sat back down, watching the second hand on the clock. Then she finally said, "I'll tell you two things I know, and then I'm not saying nothing else because I don't know nothing else, and the only reason I'm telling you this is because I owe it to you for the money, and it's something good about Del. Then you got to take me to the bus. Okay?"

"Okay," I said, wondering what good thing she could possibly say about a man like Delmundo Real.

"I heard Del tell this dude that his client didn't do Jayne and Layne," she said. "He said the man did Iris, but he didn't do Jayne and Layne. He said it just like that, and I believe him too because Layne and Jayne didn't work for Del like me and Iris did. I ain't telling you nothing else, because I told you all I know," she said. I accepted it even though I knew that she hadn't.

I gave her my pepper spray and the Swiss army knife before we left for the bus. But she'd need a hell of a lot more than that if Delmundo Real came looking for her in Atlanta. When we walked through the lobby, I walked behind her, making sure that nobody followed us. When we got to the station and she went to buy her ticket, I slipped a woman with an easy smile and a trustworthy face fifty bucks and asked her to keep an eye on "my daughter" until she got to Atlanta, and she promised that she would. I prayed she would keep her word.

"I'm starting to see the other side now. It's almost like none of this even happened to me," Amaretta said as she gathered her things and prepared to get on the bus, and I thought that she probably was. I'd bought her a couple of paperback romances, along with *Essence, The Source* and *Vibe*. She did look better, more relaxed and less afraid. Amaretta Jones was a "tough little cupcake," as my brother Johnny would have put it. A stone-soul survivor. I tried to imagine a good future for her as we stood there together: a peaceful life with her brother, good friends and a college diploma. The life her aunt—and her mother— dreamed that she would lead. It would be a safe, happy life where she could strut out of college in her blue cap and gown, with ambition, direction, and those classy little pearls in her pretty brown ears.

"By the way, who gave you those earrings?" I asked as she got in line for the bus.

"My mama. Her daddy gave them to her when she finished high school. She just put them in my ears one day and told me to wear them before something bad happened to them." She touched them delicately with her finger, the way she probably did whenever she thought about her mother. I grabbed her and gave her a hug.

"Take care of yourself, little girl," I said, and then I remembered to ask her what had made Rook so mad at her.

She shook her head and gave a loud, fast-girl suck of her teeth.

"All I was doing was trying to fix up things between Gabriella and her brother Carver. I figured that if I could make up with Vernon, she could make up with Carver and whatever he had done to her was probably no big thing. So I called his family's place down here and left a message telling him where he could find her."

"And Rook freaked out over that?"

"Yeah." She shook her head incredulously. "He started screaming and crying and carrying on like some kind of a fool, and the next thing I knew he was running down the street talking about warning her like he'd lost his damn mind. All I did was tell her brother something he really wanted to know."

We both shook our heads, puzzled by Rook's overreaction, and I stood on the corner grinning and waving at her bus as it pulled off. It wasn't until I was headed back to my car that the significance of what she'd just said struck me.

14

"**D**on't do this," Gabriella Desmond said in the scared, shrill voice of a little girl. "Put the gun away."

"But you said you wouldn't tell. It was a secret. You promised!" Carver Desmond's voice broke like that of a boy on the verge of manhood. I listened to them argue through a partially cracked door as they played a scene that hurled them back into their childhood, one that was both intimate and forbidden.

"I didn't tell."

"You did!"

"I didn't!"

"But they'll know anyway when the baby comes."

"No, they won't. How could they know that?"

"You told Rook," he said. "You told him, didn't you?"

"Just about our baby. Not about the other thing. Not what you told me not to tell."

I was repulsed yet mesmerized. It was the final piece of a puzzle that hadn't fit together until now. I'd had everything right but the perpetrator; she was pregnant with her stepbrother's child not her stepfather's. I knew very little about sibling incest and tried to recall what I'd read. I knew that the greater the age difference between the abuser and the victim, the more violent the relationship and the more devastating the resulting trauma. I'd read somewhere that it was less damaging if siblings were young and very close in age because there wasn't the same betrayal of trust. When there were years between siblings, however, the abuse was as it would be with an adult. There were four years between Gabriella and Carver. She'd been nine when she came into the Desmond home; he'd been close to fourteen. It had ended with her pregnancy and then she'd run away from him. When and why had it started?

"Please let me call somebody to help him, Carver. He's still breathing. I need to help him before he dies."

"No!"

"But he hasn't done anything!"

"He took you away."

The apartment building where we were was squalid and nearly deserted, not at all what Dominique Desmond thought she was getting for her money. It was the kind of place where nobody knows or wants to know what's going on, where a gun could be fired and nobody would give a damn.

Blood seeped down the floor and underneath the cracked door toward me. Nausea swept me as I stepped back to avoid it. The floorboards creaked when I shifted my body, and the sound, which under most circumstances would be unnoticeable, was jarring in the silence of the hall. I froze; everything was dead quiet.

"Who's there?" His voice was trembling.

I held my body rigid, afraid to breathe.

"Go away now," he said. "Go! Whoever you are, this is none of your damn business."

I know the way desperate men sound. There is a hopelessness in their intonation, a despair that tells you they don't give a damn about anything in this world, and I heard that now in Carver Desmond's voice. He had pushed himself to the edge and he wasn't going over it alone. I listened for another sound, anything that would tell me where things stood.

"Please help me," Gabriella said. It was a pathetic cry to whoever might be out there, to anyone who could hear her.

I knew that he would kill her if I left. He would know I'd gone to get the police and that would give him the excuse he needed to finish the job he'd come here to do. I'd come back, cops in tow, and there would be three bodies lying on the floor; a double murder and a suicide. The two of them and whoever else he'd wounded.

"Rook?" Her voice was forlorn, on the verge of hysteria as she begged her friend to stay alive. She called out to him, a plaintive, frightened wail that broke my heart.

"Who's there?" Carver asked again. I knew without seeing him how tightly he must be holding the gun, how quickly he could fire it. He might fire through the door in the next moment, shoot me and any chance they had would be blown. I pushed the door open, stepped inside, took my chances.

"It's me, Tamara Hayle." I spoke calmly, reassuringly, in the way I'd learned years ago to quiet a deranged person. "Let me help you, Carver. Let them go, and everything will be all right." I took a step forward, and then another, easy and slow, taking everything in.

The room was dim because the shades had been pulled, and daylight broke into it only in streaks through the torn shades. A tattered striped couch was pushed against the wall. A broken-down kitchen table littered with McDonald's french fry bags leaned against a corner. Canned laughter from some inane sitcom poured in from a TV in another room. It occurred to me that sound might be the last one I heard in life.

Carver Desmond stood in the middle of the floor as straight and tall as he had the day I met him—everybody's favorite son, the pride of a proud family. He was dressed preppy style as I had seen him in the casino that night with Jayne Lucindo: herringbone pants and microsueded brown shirt. But his clothes hung off him like those of a scarecrow. His face was unshaven and pale. His arms were stiff and the gun at his side looked like an extension of his hand.

Gabriella Desmond wore nothing over her pregnant body but the *FUBU* football jersey Rook had on when I'd seen him. She was barefoot, her toenails painted bright red. Her hair had grown out of the spike cut of her mother's photograph and formed a crown of soft black curls around her face. She was shorter than I thought she would be, and her pregnancy weighed heavily on her small-framed body. Her pretty face was filled with anguish when she gazed at me and then when she looked down at the boy who lay on the floor beside her.

Rook was sprawled out on the floor, one arm

flung above his head, the other wrapped round his body, a leg extended in a distorted version of a dancer's pirouette. He had been shot in his left shoulder, and he moaned softly; his body twitched. I glanced at the gun Carver Desmond was holding. It looked like a 22-caliber Ruger fitted with a cheap suppressor to muffle the sound. I didn't think Rook's wound was fatal, but he'd lost a lot of blood, and he was frail and in lousy shape, for a kid. There was no way to tell how long he would last if he didn't get help soon. If he was going to live, I'd have to move fast. I studied Carver's face, wondering if I could talk him into giving me the gun. Anything was worth a chance.

"It's all right," I said again. "Everything will be all right." He knew me. We'd talked before. It wasn't as if I were going into a situation like this cold. I'd been helpful to him, but I hoped he wasn't too far gone for that to make a difference. "Give me the gun, and everything will be fine. He's still alive. You're not in trouble. This was a mistake. You made a mistake. Anybody can make a mistake." The gun came up. He aimed it at me.

"You don't know what I've done," he said, and before I could lie enough to tell him that whatever he'd done didn't matter, Gabriella told what she knew.

"Why did you kill them?" She was off her knees

now, her body swaying with the weight of her pregnancy as she confronted him, her jersey covered with Rook's blood. "Why, Carver? Why did you kill them!" I tried to think of a way to signal her, to tell her to be quiet and let me handle it, but it was too late. "Why, Carver?"

I sank down into the spot where she'd been beside Rook, and he opened his eyes. I leaned toward him and told him he would be okay, even though his eyes told me he didn't believe it.

"I was just going to go away, Carver. Me and Rook were going to leave. Ma gave me money and we were saving it, and everything was going to be okay. I'd have the baby, and we could just forget it ever happened. Everything."

"I can't forget it." The gun shook in his hand. "You're the only one I ever had."

"But Jayne and Layne didn't do anything to you. They didn't even know."

"They wouldn't tell me where you were," he said quietly and so reasonably it sent a chill through me.

So Amaretta had been right. The man who had murdered the other women had not killed Jayne and Layne. Whoever he was had stuck to his pattern, after all. One a month, hiding their bodies where they couldn't be found, and Carver had fit his murders into his scheme, even to the fatal beatings. And the shot through the head had added a crazy touch, if that had been what he had intended.

My instinct had been right about Jayne Lucindo. She had recognized him when she saw him in the casino. Did she approach him later, blackmail him, tease him with information she didn't have into giving her some money? But Carver Desmond had killed her, still looking for Gabriella and now he had finally found her.

If I knew the whole story I might be able to figure a way out. Gabriella, eyes glazed, stared in my direction. She had no idea who I was or why I was here, and there was no way I could tell her now. She would have to trust me. I forced myself to focus on Carver, trying to detect any weakness or vulnerability. He was scared, too. I could tell that. But he was also a killer even though he hadn't killed Rook yet, and I wondered why that was, why he hesitated.

Gabriella still stood before him, sure of herself, and strangely enough looked like the stronger of the two, although I knew that couldn't have always been the case. It hadn't been when the abuse had started, the abuse that he thought of as love. He stared back at her, a baffled expression on his face as if he'd stumbled into a situation that he had no idea how he'd gotten into or how to get out of.

278

"It wasn't right what happened," Gabriella said, in her own way trying to reason with him, find her own way through this.

"No!"

"It had to stop, don't you know that?"

"It didn't have to!"

"I've stopped it," she said. "It's done. It will never happen again. I won't let it."

Rook stirred, moaned slightly and then called out for Gabriella, and she bent back down, taking his hand in hers. Carver aimed the gun at them both now, playing with it, looking over its barrel like a kid does imitating a gangster on TV.

Don't let him shoot. Don't let him shoot. Don't let him shoot. I repeated the words as if they were a prayer.

Without leaving Rook's side, Gabriella glared at Carver, putting all her contempt into her eyes, like a mean little girl defying a bully of a big brother who was trying to make her do something she didn't want to do. The way she must have done when she didn't want to play their "game" anymore. Or when she ran away with Rook to escape him. But he wasn't going to let her get away with it now any more than he did then.

"Get up. Or I'll kill him this time. I swear I'll kill him."

I eased close to her.

"Do what he says, Gabriella," I whispered into

her ear. "He's killed before and he has nothing to lose now. He'll kill us all if he has to. He's not the person you knew, and there's nothing you can say to stop him. Do what he says."

She began to tremble. I put my hand on her shoulder to steady her.

"What did you tell her?" He directed the gun at me again, and my heart beat in my throat. I took a deep breath in through my nose, not opening my mouth so he couldn't see how scared I was.

"I told her to do what you said." He dropped the gun to his side again. I noticed the slashes on his hands that I'd seen that morning in the casino; some hadn't healed yet, and some were new, as if made very recently. I kept my eyes focused on him with sudden, terrible insight.

He had said hardly anything to me since I'd entered. I had come in, bent over Rook, whispered to Gabriella, and it was as if I hadn't been there. It was being played out between the two of them, between him and his stepsister about the relationship that had led them to this. I didn't exist for Carver Desmond, but I knew he couldn't let me live. But he was stronger than I was, and it was ridiculous to think I could take the gun away from him. I remembered the strength in his hands. He would finish off Rook, Gabriella, me and then himself. That would be the way things would go down.

I want to disappear. Like my mother did.

I recalled his words that day in the casino. Was this his way of finally joining her?

Laura the librarian had said something about his mother, and finally it came to me.

Dorothea would just wring her hands and cry because she was so unhappy. The only thing that brought her joy was her boy, Carver. She used to call him 'Manny,' used to say he was her little man.

Fear is a stimulant. It makes everything come clearer, sharper, as my thoughts were coming now, and another one came. The first day we met he mentioned something about his mother and I tried desperately to remember it. It had been something about mothers and protection, offering protection, not giving protection. At the time I'd thought he was talking about Dominique, but could it have been his own mother, Dorothea? Had she failed to protect her son from somebody intent upon hurting or frightening him? I remembered the words in the autobiography that Carver Desmond had written. Had he chosen to satisfy those "base urges" he wrote about in his autobiography "swiftly and secretly" with a little boy? Could that dead evil man be the source of Carver Desmond's rage and perversity?

"I'm tired," he said. "So tired." His voice had changed suddenly. It was higher, softer, almost feminine. Something had changed in his attitude, too. A certain carelessness, as if he were tired of waiting for something to happen, and I knew that things were coming to a conclusion, and I was afraid of what that end would be.

"Please let me go." Gabriella sensed it, too. She was ready now to plead for her own life and that of her baby. But he wasn't listening. He pointed the gun in her direction, giving her his answer with that motion. He would never let her go. Not from this room. Not from his life.

I took a chance, gambling on a notion because it was the only thing I had.

"Your uncle is dead. He's gone, Carver, and he's burning in hell for what he did to you." He turned to me, staring at me in disbelief.

"He made you keep it a secret, but secrets like that destroy. Your mother took her own life because she couldn't protect you, because she loved you so much she was ashamed that she hadn't been able to take care of you. And you will honor the memory of your mother, your love for her, by letting us go. By freeing us as she would have wanted you to do."

The look in his eyes told me I'd made a terrible mistake. His hand began to tremble so violently he couldn't hold the gun steady, and I was thankful for that because the shot he fired in my direction missed me, but the sound went through me like a bullet would, and I crumbled to my knees, my hands covering my face. Rook moved and moaned again. Gabriella fell to the floor next to him, covering his thin body with her own. When Carver spoke, his voice was hushed, yet his words were some of the clearest I'd ever heard in my life.

"My uncle Carver died when he found out our secret. The secret Mother and I kept together. The secret way we loved."

Everything was still. Nothing moved. There was no sound in the room. A child's voice called from somewhere down the street, tires squealed as a car driving fast rounded a corner, music played from somewhere, soothing, beautiful music, and I closed my eyes and took it in, brought it into my soul to nullify the words he'd just spoken. It came together for me then, all of it with its terrible truth, which he had concealed from everyone except Gabriella.

The horror of what she had done had killed his uncle, and his mother's guilt had made her take her life. And that had left Carver, her little man, her Manny, to carry their shame through his life. He had abused his new sister in the same secretive, destructive way in which he had been abused by his mother. But Gabriella had escaped, and he'd gone looking for her, the only one who knew his secret, murdering the women who wouldn't betray her, girls with long hair and fair-skinned complexions who looked like his mother—his first love and abuser, Dorothea Desmond. He had tried to kill the dead, beating the life from them and then shooting them in the face, obliterating his mother every time he did it.

"I loved you," he said to Gabriella.

She stood up, back straight, and shot her words into his face. "I hated you," she said. "I hated you because of what you did to me, because of how you used me, because of the shit you've put me through, and I will always hate you." She wavered slightly as if she might fall, and I stood up to catch her, but she pulled her body in, making herself strong. "But I have forgiven you because I am going to have this baby, and I can't afford to carry my hatred for you inside me for the rest of my life."

Her voice had dropped to a whisper meant only for him to hear. She spoke with the assurance of a full-grown woman, and I knew that nothing in this life could ever defeat her again. Carver Desmond knew it, too.

"Please don't leave me," he begged her one last time.

She turned her back on him and closed her eyes.

He walked backward four paces, unaware of what was behind him or beside him. He smiled once in Gabriella's direction, a shy, teasing smile that turned up the edges of his mouth, cleared his throat as if he wanted to make a statement, and then put a bullet through his head.

I understand the legacy suicides leave. But victory is always with the living, and I thought of that as I sat with Gabriella on the floor holding her hand as she held Rook's. Someone had finally called the police. We waited for them to come.

"Do you know why I want to keep this baby? Why I'm not going to kill it like everybody wants me to?" she asked me after a while. She put her hand on her womb and then took mine and placed it there, too. I could feel the gentle movement of her baby inside her. I said a silent prayer for whoever he or she was.

"I want some good to come from this bad. My baby will be fresh and good when it's born, you know what I mean? Like spring when it beats out winter or clothes when you take them out of the wash. My baby is going to make every dirty thing I've lived through pure." She spoke with all the certainty in the world, and I believed her.

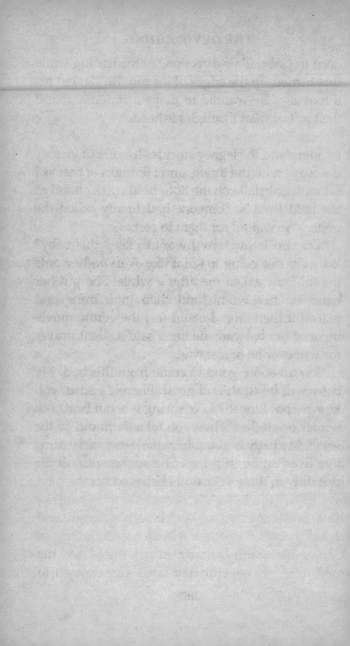

Epilogue

Carver Desmond's suicide brought my brother's death back to me, and I was overcome by sadness and grief. My guilt was overwhelming, too. I'd guessed wrong about the father of Gabriella's baby and the person who had abused Carver Desmond and those false assumptions had nearly cost people their lives. My belief in my instincts and abilities as a P.I. were shaken as they'd never been before. Basil called me when I got back to my hotel that night, and I spent the next week with him. The first day I did nothing but sleep, the next two days I cried. Finally I was able to talk, make love, remember how good it felt to laugh and close my eyes without that last haunting image of Carver Desmond burning in my brain. On the morning of the seventh day, I was sane enough, at last, to face my son. I was still in bed and Basil was showering when a photograph of Delmundo Real appeared on the news.

He was identified simply as a gambler with well-known ties to organized crime in several countries. He had been shot to death, and his assailant was unknown. There were no clues, leads or witnesses. The police assumed he'd been killed by someone within his organization. The story was followed by a report about the gala opening of a new casino, but I heard nothing; I was too stunned. Basil came into the bedroom, his skin still damp from the shower, beads of water sparkling in his hair. A fluffy white towel was flung around his neck, another tied around his waist. He slipped that one off and pulled on his black briefs.

"So you'll never have to worry about him again," he said. He went to his closet, selected a shirt, trousers, socks and tossed the clothes on the bed behind him. I watched him, hypnotized by the grace with which he moved and the beauty of his body. He glanced my way and smiled in the enchanting way he always did, then his eyes filled with concern. "What's wrong, Tamara?"

I wasn't sure myself, except I had a sudden, uneasy feeling about the way the man had died. My thoughts were too vague to explain, but I needed an answer from Basil, some kind of an explanation.

"Did you have anything to do with it?" I asked.

"With what?" His eyes were innocent.

"With his death."

"Me?" He looked shocked and genuinely hurt.

"Yes."

"What would make you think such a thing?" He smiled his charming smile, put on his shirt, scrutinized its fit, then glanced in my direction, waiting for my answer.

"Because you hated him."

"Many people hated him." He sat down beside me on the bed. I caught a hint of his cologne, and the memory of our lovemaking an hour before swept through me like wildfire. "It was probably someone he knew. Who else could get that close?"

"Did you kill him?" I didn't know if he was lying and that bothered me.

"Listen to me, Tamara. Don't mourn his death. You're safe now. You would have been next, don't you know that? Because of your connection to both me and the girl you saved. Two birds with one stone, he would have called it. It was clear to me the moment I saw your car that sooner or later, he would kill you, your son, your friend, anyone who was dear to you or to me." He stood up, pulled on his trousers, tucked in his shirt, zipped them up, slid his thin leather belt through the loops.

"Did you do it?" My voice was louder, shriller

than I meant it to be. I wasn't sure how to gain control of it.

He glanced at me in surprise, then shook his head in seeming frustration. "Think what you will, my love, but don't trouble yourself about it." He selected a pair of shoes from his closet, sat down on the bed, slipped on his socks and pulled them on.

"Did you kill him?"

He took my hands in his and held them gently. "If I told you the truth, would you believe me?" he asked and gave me a last tender kiss.

So Basil and I went our separate ways as we always do, at least until our paths cross again, and I returned home, to my son, broken skylight and all the little worries and joys that make up my life. He was right about one thing, though—I was safer because Delmundo Real was dead, and so were Jamal, Amaretta and all the helpless victims he offered to those who could pay him.

I was richer, too, thanks to the Desmonds' check—and older and at least a little wiser, as I usually am in the end. And when I think about those days in Atlantic City with all their sorrow and tragedy, I remember Gabriella Desmond's faith that her baby would cancel out all the terrible things she'd been through and make the world as fresh and good as she dreamed it could be. I pray she will be right.

Coming soon in hardcover
from #1 *Blackboard* bestselling author
Valerie Wilson Wesley

Always True To You
In My Fashion

Available in Fall 2002
from William Morrow
wherever books are sold